matters arising

from the identification of the body

a guerline scarfe investigation

simon petrie

Typeset in Adobe Garamond Pro / Candara
Cover artwork by Lewis P Morley
Cover and internal design by Simon Petrie

National Library of Australia Cataloguing-in-Publication entry

Title:	Matters Arising from the Identification of the Body / Simon Petrie.
ISBN:	9780648322801 (pbk.)
Subjects:	Science fiction, Australian.
	Crime fiction, Australian.
Other Authors / Contributors:	
	Harvey, Edwina, editor.
Dewey Number:	A823.4

matters arising

from the identification of the body

simon petrie

books by simon petrie

(the titan sequence)

Matters Arising from the Identification of the Body

Wide Brown Land

A Reappraisal of the Circumstances Resulting in Death (forthcoming)

Flight 404

Murder on the Zenith Express: the Gordon Mamon collection

80,000 Totally Secure Passwords That No Hacker Would Ever Guess

For Owen and Bill

who won't, alas, get to read it

prologue

She took her helmet off.

That's where it starts; that's where it ends. That's all there is.

If there was something to explain it, would such an explanation help? I doubt it. But there is nothing, no note, no message, no final transmission.

There's just one last, desperate deed.

She took her helmet off.

There's footage. I should not have viewed it. I cannot now erase the sequence from my mind. But I was not strong enough: I craved, with an urgency stronger than any thirst, one last sight of her alive. I needed it.

It was a grim mistake, a big bad mistake. I did not need it.

The footage does her no justice. Nor does it answer anything.

She steps away, just far enough from the main north personnel hatch to be beyond easy reach of rescue. She turns and faces the cams she must know are watching. She watches back, her thoughts unreadable, unguessable through her half-mirrored visor. Not even her facial expression can be discerned, but her body language, gloved hands defiant on hips, proclaims *Here I am, I know you see me*. Then she turns her head again – *but some things are private* – and does it.

She takes her helmet off. And breathes a frigid parody of air.

The footage ends there, after just a couple of long seconds of the onset of cold-shock paroxysm. But I've read the reports – how could I not? – and so I know, my mind's eye sees, what comes next.

She's still alive, sprawled like a beached fish, gasping and thrashing, when, after fifty-five seconds, the rapid-response team rushes out in their blue-and-white T-suits, frantically fastens a respirator over her nose and mouth, and hurries her back into the airlock; but there's no hope for her, and they know it. She's breathed full Titan for almost a minute, it's in her freeze-wracked lungs, it's left its taint in her blood.

She endures, flailing, coughing and twitching, for a further forty minutes, while her body strives not to succumb, but it's not what you'd call "life".

It's a particularly nasty way to die.

one

She called the couple through into the clean, functional austerity of the meeting room, its sole over-large table not even personalised by anything so hospitable, so conciliatory as a cursory bowl of flowers. There'd been no time.

'Guerline Scarfe,' she announced, shaking their hands in turn. Hainan's brief grip was uncomfortably strong, more like someone half his age; Morgenstein's almost feather-soft by comparison. She directed them to a pair of plain C-fibre chairs across the table from her own.

She gave them the sympathy smile. 'My sincere condolences for your loss.'

'Thank you,' said Joshua Hainan. He took his seat with the hesitation of one convinced of too great a personal solidity for mere furniture to support.

While she dispensed water into three tumblers, Scarfe watched the pair opposite. Hainan had piercing mid-blue eyes and a sharp, prominent nose, his head adorned by a silver mane of almost shoulder-length hair. His stance, his posture, was that of a younger man, but the face looked ancient. *Too old*, she thought briefly before banishing the notion, *to be the father of a twenty-year-old*. He allowed the briefest of frowns to cross his face before settling on a more neutral expression. It was a face, Scarfe judged, that had worn a lot of frowns over the years.

Yrsa Morgenstein, in contrast – whom Scarfe had heard to be Hainan's senior by a couple of standard years – had the kind of ageless appearance few people were able to carry off, her eyes dark brown, not yet the slightest hint of crows' feet, barely even of wrinkles on her face. Full lips. Thick black hair arranged in a taut-pulled bun. (*Treatments*, Scarfe thought. People as wealthy as Hainan and Morgenstein would be well able to afford all manner of youth-extending treatments.) Some calculus of body language led Scarfe to adjudge that Morgenstein was being very careful right now with her expression, which was even more bland – more guarded? – than that of her husband.

Scarfe could not, of course, begrudge their polite resistance. Few people were ever happy to see her in her professional capacity. Pain was always there, if not erupting out onto the surface then just beneath, waiting to be abraded free.

She distributed the tumblers and nodded towards these bereaved parents. (*So far*, she thought, *so rote*.) Then she absently touched the casing of the small recording device that sat like some flattened-ovoid totem on the table in front of her. 'Perhaps it would be most helpful if you—'

Hainan interrupted her. 'Don't see at all why we need to be put through this,' he gruffed, then wormed a finger down the side of his shirt's surprisingly high-necked collar, grimacing at something. (The scratchiness of newly-printed clothes? But the shirt looked well-worn, perhaps even a small bit grubby. And though neither Hainan nor Morgenstein was clad untidily, nor, it seemed, had they made any substantial effort to dress up for this meeting.) 'An investigation's not going to bring Tanja back, is it? Much less a *chat*.'

Scarfe knew of a hundred elaborations she could have offered at this point; ultimately she settled on a simple, softly-spoken, 'No.'

She made eye contact, again, with each of them in turn, cast her eyes down briefly to the recorder in front of her, and added, in the same slow, quiet tones, 'These conversations are seldom pleasant, but they are a legal requirement, and I very much hope that you may find this one of some benefit to you at this difficult time, or in the days ahead. Within the boundaries of Fensal prefecture, all cases of apparent suicide—'

'*Apparent* suicide?' Morgenstein asked, her composure shattered. Hainan placed a reassuring hand against her arm, which visibly quivered. Hainan withdrew his hand, appeared not to know what to do with it, stared at it briefly; allowed it to sink to his lap.

'—must, by law, be investigated by a licensed forensic psychologist, with the ultimate aim, through lessons learned, of engendering a kinder, more responsive, more inclusive society. I will keep this discussion as informal and as brief as I can – though of course your questions are welcomed, should you have any – but there are certain things that, by law, I must ask you.'

'What happens to the recording?' Hainan asked, warily eyeing the device on the table.

'You'll receive an auto-generated transcript at the termination of this meeting,' said Scarfe. 'The original record will be retained on file, with access restricted to myself, the medical examiners and my supervisor while the case remains formally open. On closure of the case the file will be sealed, accessible only with permission from all parties represented. After five standard years, it will be destroyed, unless all parties agree that it be retained indefinitely. You can petition, should you wish, for it to be deleted earlier than the five-year default, but by law it must be retained for a minimum of one standard year following case closure.' She breathed in, breathed out heavily, tried to soften her expression:

the boilerplate stuff always seemed to set her face in a stern cast, no matter how she strove to circumvent it. 'I know that this… attention… can appear invasive. But I can assure you, I hope, that I have no wish to intrude on your grief.'

'You've already *done* that,' complained Yrsa Morgenstein, reaching into her pocket for a handkerchief. 'Intrude, I mean.'

'My apologies,' said Scarfe. She took a sip of water, cleared her throat. 'I'll start by asking for a brief description, from each of you, of your daughter's personality. A sense of who she was.'

'Well, there was no sign that I could pick up—' Morgenstein began.

'We'll get to those questions in a few minutes,' Scarfe cut in. 'If you don't mind. Right now, what I'm after – what the form of this conversation requires – is an insight into the essence of Tanja. What made her tick?'

'This won't bring her back,' Hainan reiterated. The statement drew a sharp sideways glance from Morgenstein, which the industrialist did not acknowledge. 'Quiet, though. She was always quiet, completely the opposite of… She kept herself to herself. I found it difficult to draw her out.'

'She was her own person,' Morgenstein elaborated, crushing the handkerchief into a ball, then smoothing it flat on her thigh. 'She had quite a broad range of interests – engineering of course, literature, photography. She taught herself piano.' She bowed her head, withdrew into herself for a few moments, though her voice remained clear. 'Piano,' she repeated, slow and careful, as though it were the strangest word in the language. 'We're not— none of us are the slightest bit musical.'

'Would you have said she was happy?' Scarfe asked, eyeing the mother, then the father. 'For some people, solitude can be a blessing – and I'm getting the sense that your daughter was a very private person – while for others…'

'I don't—' began Hainan, doing the finger-down-the-collar thing again.

'She enjoyed being who she was, I think,' said Morgenstein. 'She hadn't fully decided what she wanted to do with her life, but then—'

'There was always the hope that she would go into engineering, like her br—' Hainan stopped himself. He clumsily interlaced the fingers of both hands on the table surface in front of him. 'Engineering, to continue the family tradition.'

Scarfe nodded once, wondering at Hainan's verbal arrests. Wondering, too, at the freight behind Morgenstein's reaction to them. Yrsa Morgenstein was wiping her eye with the handkerchief, and her breathing had become heavier.

'We can pause for a couple of minutes, if you need it,' said Scarfe.

'No, let's proceed,' said Morgenstein, her voice erratic, threatening to crack. 'Please.'

Hainan glowered.

Scarfe offered what she hoped was a reassuring half-smile. 'Did she have siblings?' *There's no record on Tanja Morgenstein's file. Age, education, parents' occupations of course; prospective heiress of Hainan Global Engineering AB. Single, no health concerns beyond an episode of acute asthma as a young child…*

Morgenstein exhaled heavily. A look of utter desolation flashed onto, then off, her face. She shifted in her seat, angling away from her husband.

7

Scarfe threw a glance to Hainan.

'She had a brother,' Joshua Hainan explained. 'Piotr. He was – he was three years older than Tanja.' He looked toward – though not fully toward – the shape of his wife, who was biting her lip and struggling with some inner turmoil. 'My— our son died eight months ago, in Ligeia Mare. We'd taken him methane-diving.'

Scarfe realised, belatedly, that she had heard of this incident, the industrialist's son; she just had somehow not connected the dots to *this* Joshua Hainan, this father. 'Was that the lakesuit malfunction that was reported?'

'Not a technical malfunction, no,' said Hainan. 'Though he was diving at the time.' His voice went somewhere faraway, somewhere quiet and dead, and whatever his eyes were seeing right now, it wasn't anything in the room. 'He suffered a major brain aneurysm at a depth of around thirty metres. By the time we got him to the surface, and out of the suit, he was, to all intents and purposes, gone. We kept him on life support for the next ten days, but there was no hope for him. He was pronounced dead the night after we turned off life support, just two days after his twenty-third birthday.'

'I am so sorry to hear that,' Scarfe replied. 'You have my sincerest sympathies.'

'We were just moving past it,' said Hainan, almost accusingly. 'And now this.'

Morgenstein had not moved during the past couple of minutes. She might as well have been carved from ice. Or something yet colder.

'Were Tanja and… Piotr close?' Scarfe asked.

'They were brother and sister,' said Morgenstein, as though this answered the question.

'They were *very different*,' Hainan said, as though this provided a better answer. He paused, then added, 'They got on well, though he was always a bit too… protective, I suppose you'd say, for her liking. Piotr was always the more career-focused of the two—' He closed his eyes briefly, pressed his lips together. Frowned. Lifted his hand, almost defensively, to his collar. 'They were… comfortable around each other, provided Piotr respected Tanja's need for solitude. He didn't always.' He moved his hand to his wife's shoulder.

'You make them sound like a pair of animals at the zoo,' Morgenstein announced. She turned sharply in her seat as though trying to throw off her husband's hand. The act could not definitively be categorised as rebuff, but there was no mistaking the tone of rebuke in her voice. 'They got on *fine*. They were a good brother and sister. Yes, Piotr could get a bit loud for her sometimes, but Tanja looked up to her brother.' She lifted her hand to her chin, blinked several times in a few seconds, and glared at Guerline Scarfe. 'And talking through this with a stranger, in some impersonal meeting room, isn't going to magic them back for us. I've lost, we've lost our daughter, in *utterly tragic* circumstances, and all you can offer us is… is…' Then she seemed to fold up into herself, as though this animation was too much effort. She sighed. Some life seemed to leach out of her face, and she slumped back into a hunched posture.

'I do understand your pain,' Scarfe said. 'And the next few questions may be the most painful; and I'm sorry for that.' She cleared her throat. 'Had there been any… episodes that could possibly be construed as a rehearsal for your daughter's death? Any attempts at overdose, self-harm, any uncharacteristic risk-seeking behavior? Any expressions of willingness to, or of interest in… ending it all?'

9

She lifted up a hand, palm forward, to forestall Hainan, who looked about fit to burst. 'I don't mean in the days or weeks immediately preceding her, uh, act. I mean more historically.'

'Do you not think,' said Morgenstein, with a dangerous precision to her tone, 'that if there'd been *any indication* of that, we would have found a way to save her?'

'Please,' Scarfe began. 'I don't doubt—'

'No,' said Hainan, softly, almost apologetically. 'There was none of that.'

'Did she leave a message? Or any other form of explanation of her actions?'

'No,' said Hainan.

'Not with us,' said Morgenstein, glancing left towards the edge of the table.

'Might there be *someone else* with whom she'd left such a record?'

Hainan shook his head.

Morgenstein said, almost too softly to be audible, 'Well, there was Uchida.'

'And who is—'

'Chaim Uchida,' Morgenstein explained, then crooked a finger against her lip.

Hainan's frown intensified into a scowl. 'Uchida was her... boyfriend, I suppose you'd have to say.'

'Do you have any reason to believe that she might have left some account with this Kane?'

'Chaim,' Hainan corrected.

'… with this Chaim?' Scarfe asked.

'Well, they'd been having some difficulties recently,' Morgenstein said carefully. The next sip of her water went down the wrong way; she spent the next several seconds coughing. 'It's possible she might have contacted him.'

'But you haven't checked?'

Morgenstein just glared at her.

'We don't exactly *get on* with this Uchida,' Hainan explained.

So do you consider that the tension between yourselves and her boyfriend might have contributed to your daughter's decision? But this was the question, of course, that she could never ask directly. It needed an answer, true enough – it was begging for one – but she would have to attempt to arrive at such by indirect means. 'How long had Tanja and Chaim been… involved with each other?'

'A year. A bit over a year,' said Hainan. 'I'm not sure I can say exactly how long.'

'How would you characterise their relationship? Casual? Intimate? Obsessive? Sporadic?'

'I really don't think,' said Morgenstein. She paused to glare at her husband, who was furtively checking his chrono. 'That we're the ones best placed to answer that.'

'My apologies,' said Scarfe. 'And we're almost finished, I think. The other thing I most need to check is to ask whether your daughter, whether Tanja had a circle of friends, of peers, who might be able to shed further light on her character.' *And on her relationships.* 'She would have recently completed the third level of education?'

'She never talked about friends much,' said Hainan.

'That's not true!' Yrsa Morgenstein burst out, then, turning from her husband to Scarfe, fell silent.

Guerline waited, watched Hainan, his face implacable and challenging, then Morgenstein, her eyes downcast. But nothing new was forthcoming.

'So she did have friends? Acquaintances?' she prompted.

There was stonewalling, eye-twitch and a tight-lipped frown, from Hainan, but Morgenstein relented after several seconds. 'She didn't have many, but there were a few she was close to.'

'When *Uchida* wasn't claiming her attention,' noted Hainan.

Then there was more silence. Scarfe struggled to disguise her rising impatience. 'Do you have any names?' she asked.

The response wasn't immediate, of course. But Morgenstein finally offered three: Dorthy Singh, Zeera Kwan, Mackenzie Chavez.

'Is that all you need from us?' Hainan asked. 'If so, I'd like to finish *now*. And we'll be requesting the minimum possible retention of this recording. One year, did you say? This has just been too painful for us.'

There had indeed been further questions in Scarfe's original plan for this meeting. But she sensed there was nothing to be gained from pushing this couple further into their grief… or back into whatever domestic argument this discussion had interrupted. She thanked them, explained how they could access the transcript – though neither of them appeared interested in this – and showed them to the door.

For a moment, Morgenstein seemed uncertain of whether she would follow her husband or set out in the opposite direction down the public building's bland corridor, but she fell into line behind him.

two

Back in her office, Scarfe thought fleetingly about seeking to establish order from her desktop chaos, but her heart wasn't in it. She took her seat.

She tried to put herself, figuratively, in Tanja Morgenstein's shoes. They weren't a comfortable fit, but she had little idea, for the moment, of where exactly they pinched.

Tanja's parents either lacked any insight into the factors which had driven their daughter to take her own life – an unusual circumstance, but not unprecedented – or they knew something which they were keeping from Scarfe; this, also, would not be without precedent. It didn't, in any case, provide the investigator with anything by way of traction. One possible factor was the open animosity between the couple, but surely this could not, by itself, ever be sufficient to lead a twenty-year-old to take her own life? (Now that Scarfe reflected on it, the ill-feeling on display had principally been Yrsa Morgenstein's, directed towards Hainan.)

The squabbling parents, the suicide: which came first?

Had something else pushed Tanja to take her own life?

She pondered that for a bit; was not sure she liked the answers that occurred to her.

She picked up a sheaf of flimsies from directly in front of her, assessed their urgency, and moved them towards the desk's periphery. A glass tholin-globe – a birthday gift from years back, when 'brother' was not such a fraught word – threatened to roll off the desk's edge. She grabbed it at the last moment and carefully placed the hollow, liquid-filled ball on the patch of temporarily bare surface closest to the desktop's center, the globe's brown 'snow' swirling and slowly settling towards a miniaturised caricature of the habitat at Janssen.

Clearing her throat, she asked her slate to assemble a summary of available public knowledge on Piotr Morgenstein.

The slate's reply was almost instantaneous. *<I believe you mean Piotr Aymeric Morgenstein Hainan. Am I correct in this assumption?>*

She nodded consent. The machine chimed softly to indicate activity. After a few seconds it chimed again, displaying a sequence of flat images and true-D views. The images showed a well-built young man, with an easy, open smile and perfect teeth. The eyes were those of his father, the nose more modest: Scarfe searched for a commonality of appearance with his sister Tanja, but the siblings seemed very different. Only the shape of the face made any suggestion at common ground between the brother and the sister.

While she mused on this, the slate narrated the information it had gleaned for her.

For the adult child of such a famous family, there was surprisingly little in the public domain: date and place of birth, some assuredly-sanitised details of his early education, the briefest of bulletins on his final accident in Ligeia Mare. Nothing of significance, other than his death, had been reported in the past five years.

<Do you wish to make a permanent or semi-permanent record of these search results?> the slate asked. She was on the verge of replying in the negative when the slideshow moved to a group shot, a family photo, the four of them posed among a stand of slender trees in what looked like the upper level of Woltjer's indoor park. Maples, aspens, beeches.

'Hold,' she said, before the visual had a chance to mutate to the next image. The true-D photo was evidently several years old: while Tanja was nearly as tall as her mother, and indeed seemed a more willowy version of the Yrsa Morgenstein who stood beside her, Piotr here was a good ten centimetres shorter, though the beginnings of the well-muscled physique seen in more recent images were nonetheless apparent. But it was the parents who really caught Scarfe's attention, for while Yrsa Morgenstein looked almost identical to the woman Scarfe had met an hour or so ago (that agelessness), this was a very different Joshua Hainan: black-haired and considerably more portly.

Has he gone off the rejuvenants? she wondered, recalling the tycoon's white mane and aged face from her interview. *That would make some sense; the treatment can't delay senescence indefinitely.*

But he's still got a bonecrusher handshake, and he moves like a younger man. Still feeling the pressure to play the corporate strongman? Or compensating for his approaching infirmity?

'Image details,' she requested.

The slate complied. The image was eight years old: Piotr was fifteen, closer to sixteen, his sister thirteen. The location was indeed the arbour level of Woltjer Indoor Park: two of the trees to the right of the vista were gifts of Hainan Global to the population of Woltjer. The image was credited to Tanja Noor Hainan Morgenstein.

15

'Retain record,' she instructed. 'Semi-permanent, filed with parent/guardian interview ident TM358X, demise twinned to that ident.'

Then she requested an image search for all group views of the Hainan-Morgenstein family.

As with the bio stuff on Piotr, there wasn't much: perhaps a scant dozen true-D images, a few flat views. On a whim, she directed the slate to order them chronologically for her. This new slideshow confirmed one thing: Joshua Hainan had lost a lot of weight in the months immediately preceding his son's demise. *Health scare, perhaps?* Though there was nothing in the industrialist's clearly-sanitised bio that offered any hint of corporeal weakness. And none of this put Scarfe any closer to getting inside the head of the shy, smiling young woman on view in the slideshow, a young woman who had recently become so desperate as to seek out a thoroughly tortuous means of death. *What must she have felt, unsealing that helmet, lifting it free, casting it aside? How could anybody do that?* She grew slick-palmed just at the thought.

<Retain this too?> the slate asked, bringing her back to herself.

'Neg,' she replied. She already had images of Tanja, covering both the period before and after Piotr's death.

The death of both children in such a short span of time added more poignancy to Tanja's fate, and raised several questions which this morning's interview had not addressed. For a moment she wondered if it would be worth seeking a second interview with the bereaved parents, or an individual interview with the mother. But she suspected this would merely antagonise the participants further. And there were surely other details she could glean from this morning's dialogue, on review of the record. In the meantime…

'Official file on the death of Piotr Hainan,' she instructed the slate.

<A death certificate, now classified for reasons of corporate sensitivity, was completed at time of Piotr Hainan's death by the attending practitioner, Dr Isandro Poul Ashkenazy, who was present as a guest of Joshua Hainan onboard the—>

'I don't mean the death certificate, I mean the coroner's report.'

<No such file exists at your level of access.>

That couldn't be right. Her involvement as an active investigator into the death of Piotr's sister Tanja should have released all this material to her if she required it.

'Reason?' she asked, a touch sharply.

<The death occurred at Ligeia Mare, well beyond Fensal's jurisdiction,> noted the slate. *<And at the time of his death, and for a period of thirty-eight standard months prior, Piotr Aymeric Morgenstein Hainan had been registered as a student at Sagan West Advanced Study Institute, and naturalised as a Sagan Autonomous Economic Zone citizen, and therefore not subject to Fensal's archival information requirements.>*

Which made sense, insofar as things stood. Except it was unclear in this scenario whether the file would be maintained by Sagan Admin, or by the governing body of the Titan Northern Lakes Region. She could petition both for the file's release; but she couldn't discern whether the effort would be worth the trouble, considering that the details of her request would inevitably be relayed to Hainan and Morgenstein. It was, after all, Tanja's death she was investigating, not Piotr's.

She did, nonetheless, need more information. *Time to check on that list of acquaintances furnished by Morgenstein*, she decided.

*

None of Tanja's circle of identified friends were here in Trafton. Singh was currently off-world, interned at the oceanographic research institute on Enceladus. Chavez and Kwan were both listed at Woltjer, where the former was undergoing further studies in intelligent materials and the latter was indentured as a probationary geochemist. Uchida was stationed at Jeffreys: his current occupation was unlisted, but since Jeffreys had a reputation as a *de facto* company town, it appeared almost certain that he was somehow associated with Hainan's major plant there.

It would be perfectly feasible to conduct the interviews remotely, and in many cases Scarfe would do exactly that; but something about the Tanja Morgenstein case clawed at her, urged a more direct approach. There were nuances to this investigation, she thought, which were likely to be missed in a virt session: people were more reliably read in a face-to-face.

She placed a request with Financing, for coverage of the prospective travel costs, stressing in her rationale the high profile (and, therefore, implied importance) of the Morgenstein case, and the limited insight offered by the parental meeting. The approval came back almost immediately, meaning (she presumed) that human intervention had not been involved in the decision.

Then she set up avatar-calls to Chavez, Kwan, and Uchida to schedule a meeting with each across the next few daycycles. This would take time, she suspected: people very seldom responded promptly to such requests.

While she configured an interactive-text transmission to Dorthy Singh, her slate chimed to advise her of incoming traffic. When she prompted for specifics, though, it was revealed to be a message from Neve, not any response to her recent queries. She sighed inwardly: she didn't want to be bothering herself with any of Neve's wordy, rambling narratives right now, which of course left her feeling as guilty as always it did, and as conflicted. *I'll read it later*, she told herself, and tried to believe it. *For now I need to concentrate on the Morgenstein stuff.*

She could have reviewed the parental-meeting record, to see what else could be wormed out, or conjectured from the body language and the subtext, while it was still fresh in her mind. But she held off on this. Instead, she elected to check on the forensic medical officer, to see what had been learned from the examination of Tanja's remains.

This, again, was the sort of thing that could be conducted perfectly adequately by virt (plus Scarfe, for all her occupational focus on morbidity and tragedy, was not good with actual, physical death). On the other hand, the hospital's mortuary wing was only fifteen minutes' walk through the building, and she was well aware that she should get more exercise. *Face-to-face it is, then.*

Checking to ensure that the relevant FMO, Kim N'Diaye, was going to be on shift, she mapped out a path, placed her recorder in her bag, inspected herself briefly in the mirror and set off along the corridors.

She knocked on N'Diaye's door.

'Wait, please,' he called out, in a voice both musical and remarkably low-pitched. After twenty seconds, the door slid open to reveal the pathologist sitting at an enviably tidy desk, poring over some report. He looked up as she entered, a broad smile gracing his ruddy, rounded face. 'Guerline! Please be seated. To what do I owe the pleasure?'

She explained the purpose of her visit, downplaying the tension that had been present in the interview with Tanja's parents. He asked her if she'd like to view the body.

Not really. 'Perhaps that might be best,' she agreed.

'Right then. Let's do that.' He stood with exaggerated care, led her back to the doorway.

The pathology suite, at the edge of the hospital level, was about three minutes' walk away, though keeping pace with N'Diaye ensured that it took twice as long: the medical officer's prosthetic legs had never mastered the forward slide that was an essential component of walking briskly in a one-seventh-*g* environment. (She wondered why he hadn't opted instead for a wheelframe. Probably, she suspected, it was an identity issue.)

Along the way, he expressed his misgivings at having to perform a necropsy on one so young and, it seemed, otherwise in good health.

They reached a bend in the corridor. 'Was there anything untoward in the tox scan?' Scarfe asked.

'It's always difficult to be one hundred percent sure in cases of atmospheric asphyxiation,' replied N'Diaye. 'But certainly I would say there was nothing out of the ordinary in terms of positive results. And digestive tract contents suggest she'd been eating well over her last day or so.'

'No sign of pre-existing acute or chronic health problems, you said. What about pregnancy?'

'She wasn't,' said N'Diaye. 'Neither, though, was she a virgin.'

'Any trauma?' Scarfe asked. 'Other than, of course, damage associated with fatal exposure to a toxic, cryogenic environment.'

She fell behind the other so as to make way for a determined-looking group, none seemingly younger than sixty, all in orthopedic X-suits.

'Negligible. A couple of minor scratches on one knee, some very minor bruising on her upper arm. Marks consistent with the hazards of everyday life. The bruising's fairly recent; it's possible that it was sustained during the... incident itself, that's the side she fell on, though her suit's reasonably well-padded. And the scratches were certainly pre-existing – almost healed.'

'Are there any indications she'd been an inhalator?' Scarfe asked. The dangerous, darkly-glamorous trend had lately been popular among a certain element of the district's youth. (While a single full breath of Titan's atmosphere was not sufficient to kill, it certainly did the body significant harm, and health officials were struggling to propagate the message that damage was cumulative.)

'I can't say categorically,' replied N'Diaye. 'With this type of... action, it would be very difficult to distinguish pre-existing internal trauma from that received at the time. But I think not.'

'So you can't be sure?'

'I consider it unlikely that she was. There's no evidence of it.' N'Diaye handprinted the door at which they had arrived. 'And knowing how protective Hainan was of his heirs, I don't see her getting an opportunity to try it. Though that, I suppose, must count merely as my personal opinion, rather than my professional one, so feel free to discount it.'

They progressed into the pathology suite – cold, bright-lit, and with the faintest hint of this region's half-rotten, sickly-sweet odour. A white-coated medic worked on something small and precise at one of a row of benches along the room's left-hand side; she looked up as they entered, nodded at N'Diaye, and then returned to her task. Towards the centre of the suite, two long tables stood under strips of blued light.

N'Diaye pulled two disposable surgical masks and several gloves from a dispenser just inside the door. He led Scarfe to the farther of the two tables, handing her a mask almost as an afterthought.

A foil-shrouded figure lay prone upon the table.

Donning her disinfectant-laced mask, Scarfe's breath caught: this part always brought her back to her brother, five years ago, and it had never got any easier. (Nor, once she remembered it, did Neve's still-unread message do anything except fan the same flames.)

N'Diaye lifted the shroud off one end of the recumbent form – though the table was sufficiently cold to chill the ambient air, the Titan-taint grew perceptibly stronger – and Scarfe, clenching her jaw, forced herself to look.

Contrary to the pathologist's advice, there was some significant bruising evident around Tanja Morgenstein's nose and disconcertingly gaping mouth; these blemishes, she presumed, were the aftermarks of the respiration unit fastened, in desperation, by the paramedics to the young woman's Titan-chilled face. Aside from this, there were none of the signs of the particular death that Scarfe had been expecting to see: no cyanosis evident, no ice-burn to the exposed skin (although, of course, the real damage would lie within, to organs and tissues not equipped to bear such extremes of cold: lungs frozen and damaged beyond all ability to function, blood contaminated by trace nitriles and other inimical components of the Titanian atmosphere).

Aside from the open mouth, Tanja looked, more-or-less, to simply be at rest. Though not, in any sense, at peace.

Scarfe noticed something else. 'Was her hair like that?' she asked.

'Yes, certainly,' said N'Diaye. 'A little tidier, of course, before we commenced the... examination. But we haven't touched that.'

Tanja Morgenstein's thick brunette hair was arranged in an almost-perfect copy of her mother Yrsa's long-sported style, a high-tethered bun. It wasn't a style that Scarfe could recall seeing on Tanja: in all of the public-record images she'd seen, the daughter had worn her long hair loose. 'Perhaps for the helmet?' Scarfe mused.

'Do you wish to see the suit?' the pathologist asked, evidently misinterpreting her comment.

'Do you *have* the suit?' she asked.

'For the moment, yes.' N'Diaye gently, almost reverently, replaced the shroud over the cadaver's head. 'We'll be releasing it to her parents in two or three daycycles, once Tech is satisfied that it remains operational.'

He led her to a bank of storage lockers at the room's far end, pulled one open. He bent in a quite unorthodox manner to do this, artificial feet planted further forward than one would normally expect. Scarfe belatedly realised that, with his prosthetics, this posture was an unconscious response to his unusually high centre of gravity.

The scent of Titan from the T-suit that N'Diaye now manhandled from the locker was... not *stronger* than the fragrance that had hung around Tanja's chilled carcass, but somehow different: less sharp, more full-bodied in some manner. More disconcertingly necrotic. Scarfe stood, awkward, wondering if she should offer to help, while N'Diaye hefted the T-suit to the other table, laid it flat. He stepped back, and she edged forward to inspect the suit.

It carried little of the ingrained grime of Scarfe's own suit. Its light-blue surfaces looked almost pristine, save for the ineradicable build-up of tholins and staining at the seams between suit sections. The med-status panel on the front torso was clean, though inactivated. The name-strip "Morgenstein" on the upper left was the suit's only apparent customisation. The helmet, too, looked clean, well-maintained, and lacking in personalisation. Whatever the suit's history, it was clear that it had either been seldom-used or well cared for. It was, of course, a Hainan – a model G3-X, if she wasn't mistaken; high-end, though not the most modern. Scarfe thought it almost a decade since this model had been in routine manufacture.

Something about the suit, the capacious, slumped, hollowed carapace of a now-dead young woman, bothered her; she couldn't identify why. But ultimately, of course, it was just a suit.

'You'll want to see her clothing, too, I imagine,' said N'Diaye. 'And her jewellery.'

'Jewellery?' she asked, raising her eyebrows.

'Oh, yes,' he replied. 'She was quite decked out. As if she was going out to meet somebody.'

He returned the T-suit to the storage locker and opened another drawer. He pulled out a bulky polymer satchel and two smaller envelopes. He passed one of the slick-skinned envelopes to Scarfe. It was heavier than it looked, and carried hardly any odour.

The jewellery. A bracelet, three rings, a brooch with an ostentatiously-large cut gem. The bracelet was C-fibre, enamelled in some manner, a colourful abstract design; the rings and the body of the brooch appeared to be genuine metal, solid, shiny. Even if they were merely tinted chrome rather than the gold they aspired to, they must have had considerable value.

'The brooch is printed diamond, I presume?'

He shook his head. 'Cubic zirconia,' he said. 'Natural, as far as I can tell.'

She whistled appreciatively in response. 'That must be worth a fortune.'

'Her parents aren't short of it,' N'Diaye commented. 'Even so…'

Scarfe handed the jewellery-laden envelope back to the medic, asked to see the clothing. N'Diaye passed her the satchel.

If the garments carried any scent from their brief exposure to Titan's atmosphere, she couldn't detect it. She could, however, discern from the weight and feel of the cloth that Tanja's costume lacked the embedded self-tailoring mechanisms generally found in mass-produced or home-printed garb, and must therefore have been fitted. Scarfe was no more an aficionado of fine apparel than of jewellery – she dressed for comfort, practicality, and a sort of entry-level professionalism that, she hoped, betokened an approachability consistent with her role – but she could see, from the fabrics as well as from the discreet black tailors' labels, that the outfit in which Tanja Morgenstein had met her end was not cheap. *Nor is it the sort of thing one simply throws on at the last minute.* 'I see what you mean about dressing to meet someone,' she remarked, and the thought left her somehow more saddened, more bereft than did the simple sight of the shrouded body on the refrigerated table.

'And there's this,' said N'Diaye, passing her the final envelope in exchange for the pile of clothing. 'It was found in one of the pockets of the jacket.'

A storage token, with what she presumed was a locker number: gamma-357. She turned it over in her hands. 'Mind if I show this to my slate?' she asked.

'I don't have any objections,' said N'Diaye.

The slate took a fraction of a second to identify the storage token, which was for a locker in the stowbank immediately adjacent to the airlock through which Tanja Morgenstein had exited Trafton. 'Have you checked this locker?'

'It's not really within the terms of the examination,' he said.

'Can I borrow the token?'

He hesitated. 'I'm supposed to retain custody of all possessions until such time as they're passed back to the next of kin.'

'It might be important,' she persisted. 'She might have left a note, after all. In the locker.'

He grumbled his assent. Pocketing the storage token, she asked if there was anything else he wanted to bring to her attention.

'She was too young for this,' he said.

She didn't respond.

N'Diaye put Tanja Morgenstein's effects away. Scarfe thanked him for his assistance.

'Anytime,' he assured her, offering another of those broad, beguiling smiles. Seemingly in afterthought, he said, 'You know Runag was one of the responders?'

'Sorry, who?'

'Runag,' said N'Diaye, and then, seeing that simple repetition hasn't sufficed to trigger Scarfe's recognition, added, 'Runag Fischetti. She climbed Erebor with us. That time Lon…' His expression darkened, as with belated realisation that the ice across which he was treading was hazardous.

'Kim, that must be over a dozen years ago. I hadn't even met Sunder then. And I've never had the best memory for names.' She brought her hand to her jawline, pressed a finger against the side of her mouth. 'Yes, I remember Erebor. I thought I'd broken my wrist. And I think I remember Runag, though I'd never have succeeded in putting a name to the face. So she found Tanja?'

'She was involved in some capacity. I think she was quite shaken, as you'd imagine.'

'It must have been… I can't really imagine. Poor woman,' said Guerline, not entirely sure whether it was Tanja or this Runag to whom she was referring. 'But I had best be getting back, unfortunately. Thanks for your help. And please contact me if there's anything else you think I need to know.'

'Such as?'

'I wish I knew.'

She bade farewell to the pathologist and took a roundabout route through the corridors back towards her office.

Since her walk led her past her favourite cafeteria, she stopped for lunch.

She picked at her RealBeef salad while the slate informed her of recently-captured messages. The two in Woltjer – Kwan and Chavez – had indicated their availability for meetings on the following daycycle. This was actually sooner than Scarfe would have preferred: she had tomorrow tentatively planned out for research and review of the extant recordings, and now she must spend the time travelling.

It meant other sacrifices too. She asked the slate to contact Sunder.

'Guerline?' Her ex-partner's voice was high, a touch hesitant. 'Something up?'

I hope you're well too. 'In a manner, yes. I need to go to Woltjer – business – and I need to know if you can have Nikita.'

'When? Tonight?'

'Sorry. I know it's short notice.'

'It is a bit. Can't he accompany you?'

'To Woltjer and back, by rail? He'd be bored flat. Plus I can't, anyway. It's *business*, Sunder. Discussing a deceased. Not fun, not something I get to choose. Can you do it?'

'It's *very* short notice. Gwer, I had *plans*. How long have you known?'

She forced herself not to react to the tone of complaint – worse, of accusation – in his voice. *Bygones*, she told herself. 'Only about five. Believe me, this isn't my first preference either. I just need an *answer*, Sunder. Yes or no. Can you?'

'This just one night we're talking about?'

'Better make it two.'

'Two? Gwer…'

You're always saying you don't see enough of him. 'I'll need to leave late today, so I'll bring Nikita round after dinner. If that suits.'

'I don't exactly have a choice, do I?'

You always have a choice, Sunder. 'Thank you.'

'Yes. Next time, perhaps a bit more notice, okay?'

'Of course.' *You could try to sound more enthusiastic. He's your son too. Or have you forgotten?* 'I'll be round later, then. Make sure he does his homework. Thanks again.' She ended the call.

Better make sure I get something to make it up to Niki, she thought, as she headed back to her office.

*

There were some gaps in the 'family details' section of the Tanja Morgenstein case proforma, which was just the kind of thing Kalinda always nitpicked about. Seeking to address this, Scarfe had hoped that an enquiry to Yrsa Morgenstein would prove more productive than the abruptly-terminated call she had placed, not five minutes earlier, with Joshua Hainan. But Tanja's mother's face, as the slate's static, serene image of *then* was replaced by the animated, guardedly hostile *now*, suggested this was a vain hope. Indeed, Scarfe was almost certain that she hadn't reached Yrsa herself, merely a high-functioning avatar. It quickly became apparent that this synthetic, virtual go-between, which had evidently been instructed to rebuff attempts at personal contact, was not for turning: Scarfe's questions were met with refusals to comment. She closed the call and stared in momentary defeat at the slate's screen.

Her pondering took her nowhere useful, so she tried another tack, and had the slate once again attempt to run to earth Runag Fischetti, the responder whom Kim N'Diaye had identified as a mutual acquaintance.

'Fischetti?' The screened visage was youthful, somehow impish, spike-haired; Guerline recognised it immediately, though in her memory the hair was a bright visibility-blue rather than the more restrained mid-brown it was today.

'Runag?' Scarfe asked. 'Hello. This is Guer—'

'Guerline!' Fischetti replied, breaking into a grin so apparently spontaneous that Scarfe felt an uncomfortable guilt in her own inability to have placed a name to the face. 'Uh – is this a social call?'

'Hardly, I'm sorry. But I can appreciate you're probably busy. Is this a good time?'

'If you could call back in seventy minutes, that'd be better – I'll be on a scheduled break then.'

Scarfe closed the call, looked askance at the formwork on her desk. She knew she should be making progress with the backlog, but it didn't appeal.

She needed a walk. *Maybe I can learn something useful.*

She picked up the storage token.

three

Everybody had their own description for the smell of Titan – or for the particular representative of its odours with which they were most familiar – and Scarfe's was bleached sewage. The stowbank hall, situated close to the main north personnel lock and used mainly for the storage of frequent-user T-suits, stank of it, not overly offensively but persistently; not the sharp sour smell of Titan's air, quickly dispelled by extractor fans, but the burnt-mould-and-hot-metal taint of tholins that could take months to fade. Uncleaned suits: the stowbank must see a lot of them.

It felt strange to be standing here at the stowbank's entryway, in easy sight of the airlock through which Tanja Morgenstein had walked to her end: there was nothing exceptional about the rather dowdy and depressing lock hatch, its hazard markings worn and stained by frequent use; nothing to suggest complicity in a young woman's death. But that was death for you, it hid itself well, it had no need to advertise itself. Here, those few days ago, the responders must have rushed out, with no time to think about what they might find; must have hurried back in with their precious doomed cargo; must have been met, probably in that very foyer, by others of their number equally feeling the urgency to save, using all of the experience and technology at their disposal, the life of a woman who apparently no longer wanted it and would not, in any case, manage to keep it. Of all this fevered activity, no residue, no ghost remained. Just a lost-looking businessman in the stowbank hall, reading the posted "Terms and Conditions" then staring helplessly at the token in his hand. One of the stowbank hall ceiling's three rows of lumopanels was flickering and fizzing.

The stowbank locker, large enough to store a T-suit plus a full consignment of baggage, was one of perhaps two hundred in the hall, stacked three rows high against all available walls. The locker was almost empty, containing only a small fragrance cone, fighting a losing battle against the hall's prevailing aroma; a pair of strappy, black-shiny shoes; and a slender resealable padded envelope. Scarfe removed and cursorily inspected the shoes – like the rest of Tanja's outfit, they appeared to have been constructed rather than printed – and replaced them within the locker. The envelope only held clothes: a brocaded peacock-blue cheongsam made, Scarfe thought, of silk and carefully folded, and a pair of grey linen trousers, lighter in hue than the ones which Tanja had worn beneath her T-suit, rolled to form a squat fabric cylinder. Scarfe carefully checked the garments for pockets, finding none, then folded them back up as best she could.

On her way back from the stowbank, it occurred to her that she'd be passing close to the hospital sector at the time Runag Fischetti had nominated for contact. She had the slate enquire, avatar-to-avatar, whether a face-to-face meeting would be acceptable.

'Not on the suit team, no,' said Fischetti. 'I was part of the primary decontam, once they had her inside. Stayed with her throughout. What was it, exactly, you were wanting to know?'

I wish I knew, thought Scarfe, who had remained standing despite Fischetti's invitation to take a seat. Though she had by now recollected enough of her earlier (slight) association with the other, she had been thrown, to a significant degree, by her accent, which carried an unfamiliar and entirely unremembered lilt quite distinct from the customary Trafton twang. 'Really, I'm seeking for any insight you can offer into the vic— into Tanja Morgenstein's state of mind when she was brought in. And I'm sorry, this feels really ghoulish and cruel asking you to work through this for me, so close after the incident… but I know this kind of thing doesn't generally make it into the medical reports. And in cases like this, where the deceased hasn't left a note—'

'Wasn't there a note? I could have sworn she said…'

Scarfe's eyes opened wider. 'I'm sorry, what? She mentioned a note?'

'I think she did,' said Fischetti. 'That is, I think she *tried* to. But her throat, her lungs, she wasn't in a good way at all. Poor kid. She…'

'I am so sorry to be putting you through this.'

'No, it's okay. I just, she was struggling so *hard*, you know? So hard against it. As though she'd changed her— changed her— ' Fischetti closed her eyes, breathed unevenly through her nose for several exhalations and inhalations while her closed mouth quivered. Then she sighed, blinked her eyes open, and continued. 'And that's what made it so hard, you know? I mean, you work in a hospital, it's just not possible to save every patient. But that poor kid… she'd changed her mind, and it was just too fucking late.' She blew her nose noisily. 'I'm sorry.'

The lilt, Scarfe noted, was gone; the twang was back. She waited, feeling like a heel, asking difficult questions in another woman's office.

'I've forgotten what I was going to say,' Fischetti confessed.

'The note?' prompted Scarfe.

'Ah. Yes. I can't be completely certain, but I think, I *think* that towards the end, after she'd realised she wasn't going to make it, that she said "Make sure she gets the note".'

'"Make sure she gets the note." Tanja Morgenstein said that? To you?'

'I was closest, so yes, to me I guess. But she was really having trouble getting the words out – I could be wrong. And I didn't mention it in my report, partly because I was unsure and partly because it's not my place. If there's a note, Pathology would find it. You're saying they didn't?'

'Yes,' said Scarfe. 'No note.'

'Then I must've been mistaken. But that really did sound like what she was trying to say. She was trying so damned hard, but her throat… Or she maybe left a note at home?'

'Her parents said not. You said you thought she'd changed her mind?'

'Yes.'

'That's… well, that's awful.'

'Yes.'

Scarfe thanked Fischetti for making time to see her. They chatted in a noncommittal fashion for a few minutes, comparing notes on mutual acquaintances: a stilted, precarious conversation in which Scarfe suspected that both were on guard. They promised to keep in touch. Then Scarfe left.

Make sure she gets the note. Had those been Tanja's actual words? And if so, who was 'she'? Yrsa Morgenstein?

She placed a call to N'Diaye. 'Kim, it's Guerline again.

Just checking, you did say that there was no note with Tanja Morgenstein's effects?'

'That's correct. No note. Why?'

'Just something Runag mentioned. It's probably nothing, but I thought I should double-check. Don't worry about it.'

Scarfe closed the call, hesitated, then turned around, almost colliding with a blade-skating youngster. *I need to take another look at that storage locker.*

Her second, more exhaustive inspection of the locker's contents yielded nothing that she had not already suspected from the first. No note, no databud, nothing that screamed "Read Me". If Tanja Morgenstein *had* left a note, it wasn't in this locker.

She needed to get back to her office.

Something about the clothing in the locker sparked a sense of half-informed recognition. *Have to find some way of checking on that,* she told herself as she walked. *No idea how, though.*

She realised, also, that she should have checked when the cubicle's hire was set to lapse. *I'll need to make sure her parents are kept informed of her effects.* But she was, for now, strangely reluctant to renew contact with either Hainan or Morgenstein, even avatar-to-avatar.

She tried to convince herself that this was because she was busy.

They took the chute down to the sub-basement level. The lighting down here seemed brighter, the walls clad in active, colourful, ever-changing murals. Propulsive background music attempted to distract from the thrum and rumble of the habitat's plant, buried even further below. Nikita's enthusiasm and energy, too, was infectious. Guerline still hadn't told him where they were going, but his speculation remained only slightly below fever pitch. He loved Sub-B.

'Is it one of the Weather Rooms?' he asked, his whole face making the question, as they walked – he clearly wanted to run – past a jungle scene filled, for the moment, with a raucous flight of virtual macaws. 'Jodi told me about a snowball fight his family went to last week, it sounded really spesh. And Hansel was there when they did a rainstorm—'

'No, Niki, we're not going to the Weather Rooms. Maybe another day.' She rearranged the carrysack's thin strap, which was digging into her shoulder. 'I thought today we'd go to the pool.'

'You mean the nitrogen pool?'

Scarfe sighed, as another of Nikita's repeatedly-expressed enthusiasms resurfaced. But lakesuit hire was expensive; and from what she'd heard, they didn't actually give you very long in the liquid-nitrogen-filled playzone. 'No, Nik-Nik, just the regular pool. The water one.'

His voice dropped a note or two. 'Oh. Well, that's fun too.' And she knew she'd just failed some small test.

At the pool, she prepared to take him into the adults' changing zone, but he announced he was ready to use the children's facilities; he was in fact so eager to assert his new independence that she had to remind him he'd need something to change *into*. So he waited, with that mixture of "dutiful" and "impatient" that only the young can master, while she retrieved his costume and towel from the carrysack.

'I brought your flippers,' she told him, and the smile with which he greeted this news seemed out of proportion. Then he was gone, bustling towards the children's changing area. The safety-bot played at blocking his entry, sliding left then right, but he laughed, feinted, and dodged past it. He was in.

To watch him, she mused, was to feel both young and old yourself.

He was already poolside, flippered and face-masked, when she emerged from the changing zone. At the first sight of her, he smiled and stepped off the side, attempting a fast walk across the water's surface. He got two-and-a-half paces out before overbalancing; toppled with an exaggerated theatrical gesture; and came up snorting, laughing, and coughing.

Scarfe slipped more carefully into the pool, bracing against its mild chill. She paddled over in her son's direction (really, she should take the effort to learn to swim, it'd be more enjoyable exercise than the X-suit), to be met – courtesy of the flippers – by a slow-falling spray of water.

'Niki,' she said later, as, damp-haired and cold-limbed, they took the chute back up to home level, 'I need to go away on work for a couple of days. Are you right with going back to Dad's tonight, after dinner?'

'Yes, that's okay,' he replied. 'What's for dinner? Can we have sharkstix?'

'We'll see,' she said. *Only if I can't steer you towards something more balanced.*

She should be grateful, she knew, that he was so accepting of change, of parental disruption; but would it be too much to ask that he sometimes display a concern about which parent he spent time with?

There was both a sense of freedom, and a hollowness, to having a domestic space to herself. The rooms rang with the absence of Nikita, as though there was still a ghost of him, a negative-space boisterousness, left in his wake. And for all that it was insubstantial, it left a stronger sense than the slowly-dissipating aroma of their shared dinner.

She grew inured to it; the emptiness faded, as it always did; the guilt gathered, like drifts of dust, as it always did. It was easy to lose focus without the expected distraction of her son; she needed to keep moving.

four

The ghost-smudge of crescent Saturn, hovering not quite halfway up the sky, provided thoroughly inadequate lighting for the looming dunefields that stretched from west to east along the northern horizon for the first couple of hours of the railpod's travel. Sparse clusters of illumination – habitats, vehicles, worksites – provided the only real indication that the region the pod traversed was not a barren, featureless wasteland. But these occasional interruptions of colour and activity seemed merely to magnify the dark-shrouded expanses of the wrinkled plain that separated them.

While Guerline Scarfe generally enjoyed the journey between Trafton and Woltjer – it was a trip she made a few times each standard year, for family reasons – it seemed a waste to be taking it in the slow Titanian predawn. She had her slate, of course, so she could review, read, game, or socialise, but she did not feel drawn to any of these. She opted instead for sleep.

The rail-pod was sparsely occupied. Scarcely more than half a dozen of the thirty seats had been activated, and the other passengers were arranged in two groups – a family and, she presumed, a business team – further down the car. She instructed the slate to safeguard her, alarmed the small baggage case at her feet, and pressed back into her seat, closing her eyes.

Sleep took its time arriving. She had a memory of the ten-hour journey as almost tediously smooth, with very little fluctuation in elevation and almost no deflection from the nearly-true east-west vector that marked the separation of Trafton and Woltjer, but the experience with closed eyes was quite different. Each slight deviation, each drainage-channel bridge transit, each change in servo pitch seemed amplified by the absence of accompanying or forewarning visual cues. After perhaps an hour, while she found herself ferreting through the facts and reasonable suppositions regarding Tanja Morgenstein's suicide to no avail, she succeeded in drifting off…

… and was awoken some indeterminate time later by the recognition that the rail-pod had stopped, in a landscape of near-total darkness. Her heart raced and she was given over to something akin to dread for some seconds. The reaction was ingrained, almost instinctual: *sniff for air leak, prepare to retrieve emergency breathing-suit.*

Then she recognised that the situation was not one of danger but of precaution. The pod had simply stopped in one of the periodic lay-bys while an opposing vehicle sped past it, with a humming vibration accompanying a high-pitched, doppler-shifted whine, along the single rail that connected Trafton and Woltjer. After a few minutes, the pod resumed its smooth acceleration, but the damage was done: sleep wouldn't be back.

The slate, perhaps recognising her reluctant restlessness, reminded her of Neve's still-unread message. She scanned it without enthusiasm. The letter seemed to carry even less coherence than usual: a welter of unlinked scraps of anecdote, small personal complaints, expressed regrets, questions for which Guerline doubted any meaningful answers existed. She closed the message without any response; felt, as always, a compulsion to delete it, though there was a part of her that always found it impossible to delete any of Neve's messages.

Her mood, for the rest of the journey, was a mess of confused remorsefulness, from which she attempted in vain to distract herself. But there was almost nothing to see out the viewscreen, just a very occasional wan pocket of stained terrain – windworn boulders, barren streambeds, ice-boned ridges – illuminated by the few lights that marked the route.

Woltjer, almost fifteen hundred kilometres due west of Trafton, was more than a full daycycle behind in terms of the sun's position. The railpod had more than kept pace against the as-yet-unrisen sun, with the result that there were still many hours left, here, of the week-long Titanian night. Nonetheless, as the brown-on-black flattened dome of the settlement's original arcology loomed into view, the pod was greeted by unexpectedly bright light, apparently associated with some construction occurring around Woltjer's eastern terminus. Scarfe was able to watch, for several seconds, as a twelve-metre-tall prefab cube, wrapped in protective sheathing, was cautiously manoeuvred by a large industrial crane towards an apron of recently-flattened terrain. It was yet further evidence of Woltjer's ongoing arcological sprawl.

Scarfe wondered just why it was that some settlements, such as Trafton, were able to develop within the (admittedly generous) confines of the original habitat, while others such as Woltjer and Sagan spilled out well beyond their earlier limits. (Of course, the opposite problem existed also: she'd visited habs which had gone moribund once whatever the locational incentive for their construction or continued existence had ceased. This, she supposed, was a phenomenon which would only accelerate once Sagan's elevator was operational, obviating the need for much of the present-day launch activity on which Woltjer, in particular, depended.)

Once the pod stopped, there was the habitual several minutes' delay while the disembarkation tube bridged the gap to mate with the pod's airlock. The hatches opened, with an inevitable slight ammoniacal whiff of 'outside', and she followed the business team into the station building. (The family, it seemed, was travelling on to Hunten, a further significant stretch west along the rail.) The station was moderately busy, with staff, several passengers, and one optimistic busker.

Scarfe took a few minutes to remind herself of her bearings, then made her way up the escalator and into the heart of Titan's second-largest city.

There were a couple of hours remaining until her appointment with Mackenzie Chavez. She stopped at an Indo-Creole restaurant on the second-level concourse, choosing carefully from its all-night breakfast menu. Then she found a medpoint dispensary for some pharm: her neck was sore after her sleep on the pod's seating. And a playshop, where she spent more credit than she'd prefer – guilt – on a cryocrawler kit for Nikita, who was big on vehicles right now.

At least, she hoped he still was.

On a whim, she bought another kit, a smaller one, for Freyne, though she'd promised, not that long ago, not to encourage this. More guilt.

There was a cluster of tables and seating surfaces at the edge of the concourse. She sat, waiting for the derm-patch to take effect, and used her slate to catch up on any comms traffic. There was a reply request ("important") from her supervisor, but she was almost certain

Kalinda would be off-duty by now – their respective shifts had only a couple of hours' overlap each standard day – and "important" was a grade or two below "urgent". She deferred it, with a sense of compromised relief. *Tomorrow's soon enough to pay the piper.*

Of the remaining messages, there was nothing consequential. She prompted her avatar to remind Uchida of her own earlier request, for which she was still awaiting a response.

Then, rechecking the address for Chavez's residence, she realised she'd need to move quickly if she was to make the appointment.

Mackenzie Chavez, it transpired, still lived with her parents, in a larger-than-standard new dwelling-space halfway along what Scarfe suspected was the same radial arm she'd seen the latest extension added to a few hours earlier. The corridor, at least, had the same 'modular' look to it, with retracted-bulkhead warning signs every twelve metres or so. The Chavez residence, on the left hand side of the corridor, occupied the entire span between two such bulkheads, and (to judge from the lift-platform which was one of the first things she saw when the door was opened to her) must run to at least a second storey.

Scarfe wondered what the Chavezes did for a living. An apartment such as this, located close to the admin precinct and designed for a panoramic view of the stained-ice-strewn landscape to Woltjer's north, couldn't have come cheap.

Mackenzie's mother, Huong, was the one who came to the door after it had been opened by the house servitor. Huong Chavez, dark and short-haired, with brown eyes possessing definite epicanthic folds, was so diminutive – Scarfe had almost thirty centimetres' height advantage over her – that the investigator at first mistook her for a child, and barely realised her error in time.

Scarfe introduced herself, and briefly stated the purpose of her visit.

'Yes,' said Huong. 'It's remarkable, isn't it, how possessive Fensal is of its citizens.'

'I would have said "protective",' said Scarfe, bristling inwardly.

'Oh, of course, and I mean you no disrespect at all – we all need to make a living.' Huong Chavez smiled at her, but it was a smile only of the lips. 'Won't you sit down, please? The girls will be down in a minute or so.'

Scarfe wondered at that plural as she took a seat on a slender backless chair in front of a low table veneered in what looked very like genuine wood. She wondered, too, if Huong was going to be one of those parents who, awkwardly, insisted on sitting in on their child's interview. But this, it seemed, was a needless concern, for the woman apparently considered her duties as hostess discharged, and with a curt request that Scarfe let her know if she needed anything further, retreated to a small room off the main living area. Scarfe caught a glimpse of a workstation, its viewpanel displaying a mosaic of a half-dozen low-altitude images of miscellaneous stretches of Titanian landscape, before the door slid shut.

She turned around at a noise – the lift-platform, rising towards the ceiling – and stood up shortly after, as two young women descended into the room. There was no mistaking which of the two was Mackenzie Chavez – those eyes, the same short stature – but she had no idea who was the substantially larger, black-haired woman. The two did not look like siblings, nor half-siblings. She introduced herself and extended her hand.

The larger woman shook first. 'Zeera Kwan,' she explained. 'When Mac said she was meeting you as well, I thought we may as well team up for this interview. Or is that a problem?'

'No, no problem,' Scarfe assured her, but secretly she wasn't pleased. A joint interview meant that one of the two could dominate, could influence the responses of the other: instead of two full interviews, Scarfe was concerned that she'd end up with one-and-a-half. Still, there were compensations to the arrangement – she could get instant feedback on the one's perspective, from the other, for example. And she reminded herself that these two women, just a few years out of adolescence, were struggling with the loss of someone who was apparently a close classmate; so the case for peer support was a strong one.

She'd pegged Kwan as the more forward of the two – that physical presence, a strongman grip almost the match of Joshua Hainan – but as it transpired, Chavez was in fact the more talkative, once she got going; so much so that Scarfe found herself deliberately feeding questions first to Kwan, to ensure she was getting an adequate impression of her perspective as well.

The discussion provided quite a bit of superficially-useful background information, centred largely on anecdotes relating to the girls' shared experience of Tanja's years of schooling. She asked, of course, if they knew of others of Tanja's education cohort who were close to her, and was informed only of Chaim Uchida.

'It's not that she wasn't *liked*,' said Chavez. 'I mean, nobody I know actively disliked her, except maybe a couple of the boys – but that, I think, was probably more about her perceived wealth and privilege, and they were like that with… with others as well.' A catch in Chavez's voice at this statement was enough to make plain for Scarfe the identity of at least one of those "others", but she kept the observation to herself. 'I'd say she was, on the whole, somewhat admired for what she could do. If she turned her hand to something, it was almost a given that she'd be good at it, but not rub-it-in-your-face good, if that makes sense. She never seemed to get in a spat with anyone, which is pretty surprising in some ways, considering the size of some of the personalities in our classes. But she was always a particularly private sort of person. Not in any overtly negative way, it's just who she was. And people, except for two or three of the guys, just accepted that, and went with it.'

'Where does Chaim Uchida fit in?'

'Chaim is – was – probably her closest friend, though "friend" may well be putting it too mildly. He seemed to be the one who, more than anyone, more than either of us, she would open up to. They were, I'd say they were a good match, he always seemed to be able to draw her out in a way she wouldn't allow from anyone else, and she kept him centred, maybe. If that's the word I want.'

'Were they... romantically involved?' Scarfe asked.

'It wouldn't surprise me,' Chavez offered.

'It would surprise me if they *weren't*,' said Kwan.

'But I don't think old man Hainan approved of Chaim,' said Chavez. 'I got the feeling that Yrsa, Tanja's mum, was at least neutral towards him, but Josh H, he was actively opposed. I mean he didn't stop Tanja from actually seeing Chaim, but he made sure that it was very difficult for them to arrange time alone together. And he was like that a bit, now that I recall, with Piotr's girlfriends, but nowhere near as much. Zeera told me once—'

'Thanks for dumping me *in it*, Mac,' Kwan said, though without (Scarfe thought) real heat to the barb. 'Yeah. Her dad wasn't the sort to keep an enmity to himself. I guess when you've got that much power, there's no reason to. Hainan docs have a certain reputation for ruthlessness. And no, he didn't exactly like me, and I knew it, but what I got from him was mild compared to the way he'd treat Chaim sometimes. I'm surprised Chaim put up with it, but he did. I never once saw him lose his temper with Tanja's dad. *I* would have just bopped him one. And worried about the consequences later.'

'It must have been hard for you,' Scarfe ventured, seeking to explore another strand, 'when Piotr died.'

'On several levels, for sure,' replied Kwan. 'Though he and I weren't still together by then, hadn't been for some months. It was just something deeply sad, I mean nobody deserves to die that way.'

'It must've been tremendously difficult for the family. How did Tanja cope with it?'

'How does anyone cope with it?' Chavez asked. 'She was very close to Piotr, for all that he drove her demented sometimes. I always felt that they were thrown together, by their parents' distance as much as by anything else.'

'You mean the distance between Hai— between Joshua and Yrsa?' Scarfe asked, recollecting the awkwardness of her interview with the bereaved parents.

'No, they're thick as thieves, those two,' Chavez replied. 'I mean the distance they maintained between themselves and their children. It always seemed to me that Piotr and Tanja were *cared for*, but they weren't *nurtured*. If that makes sense. As if they meant nothing more to their parents than, I don't know, a piece of sculpture or something. They didn't, their dad especially didn't, seem to make any time for them at all.'

'They're busy people, her father especially,' Scarfe argued, wondering just why she was sticking up for Joshua Hainan.

'Oh, I know *that*,' said Chavez. 'But I think it went deeper. Even that trip to Ligeia with Piotr, that Yrsa M baulked out of at the last minute—'

'Wait, she dipped out?' Kwan asked, a second before Scarfe could formulate the question herself.

'Exactly,' replied Chavez. 'She flew up to Westlake with Josh H and Piotr, then flew straight back. Said she'd succumbed to a virus, and wasn't up to an ocean voyage, but she seemed fine when Tanja and I met her at the terminal.'

'Tanja didn't go either?' Scarfe asked.

'No. Make of that what you will. But that was just typical. And what I was trying to say was, Josh H seemed resentful of taking a holiday, his own idea as far as I can tell, a holiday with his son. And I don't think that was just pressure of work.'

But the tidbit that most stuck with Scarfe was offered just before the interview's end. Kwan was relating the detail of Tanja's frustrations as a fellow photographer.

'She always wanted to focus on landscape photography,' Kwan said, in a voice that sounded remorseful.

'But she did, didn't she?' asked Scarfe. 'I mean, her public portfolio has a lot of examples of her landscapes.'

'All remote-captured,' replied Zeera Kwan. 'We arranged to go on a few shoots together, in the dunefields northeast of Trafton, but it was never *her* I went with, just a well-equipped surro. Her parents – and I know she was old enough, legally, to be making her own decisions, but it can be hellishly difficult going against someone as powerful as Josh H – her parents would never even allow her to have a T-suit.'

'But that's… I mean,' Scarfe protested, 'she was *found* in her suit. And it wasn't a new suit.'

'She never had one,' Kwan insisted, and Chavez nodded in assent. 'As far as I can remember, she'd hardly ever even left Trafton. I mean, that always struck me as very unfair. Her parents always went off all over the place, and she and Piotr were always stuck back at home.'

'But Piotr moved out, as I understood it,' Scarfe observed. 'He was in Sagan, wasn't he?'

'Well, yeah,' said Kwan. 'But that took a hell of a row with his father.'

'And even then,' added Chavez, 'even though he was thousands of kilometres away from his parents, it was still like they were in control somehow. They owned the apartment he lived in, they insisted on following and limiting his movements – if he stayed out after his studies, they'd be on his back about it. Josh H in particular.'

'And Tanja, I think, had it even worse,' said Kwan. 'I mean, they had lots of… stuff, and pretty much any kind of photography gear you could imagine, she had it. But it seemed to me that she and her brother were kind of trapped where they lived. In a way, I suppose there's no great surprise that she'd eventually find a way to rebel at that while her parents were away, but obviously none of us imagined she'd ever do anything so, so… extreme…' Kwan looked up towards the corner of the ceiling and breathed deeply. The smaller woman squeezed her friend's hand in reassurance. For a few moments it appeared that Kwan was about to weep, but that look of haunted sorrow faded from her eyes, and she placed a heavy hand on Chavez's, still holding her own.

Scarfe allowed the silence to sit a few moments, before prompting, 'So, the suit she was found in...?'

'I guess it must've been a rental,' said Chavez.

'You may well be right,' Scarfe conceded.

With her interview with Chavez and Kwan done, Guerline contemplated her schedule. There were several hours remaining before she was due to catch the rail-pod back to Trafton, since her initial travel arrangements had been predicated on a later, now redundant, meeting with Kwan. She could, she supposed, call in on her own parents; but she had been anticipating such a visit in a month or so, and the time available right now seemed scarcely long enough to justify the mental upheaval of a catch-up with her "clan". Similarly, though it would have been possible to catch up with Neve – which would have certainly discharged, for the short term, a slow-building and long-running obligation – she was reluctant to re-immerse herself in that situation just now. So, as she walked, she asked the slate to negotiate for her, if possible, a berth on an earlier rail-pod. The slate advised a departure in ninety-five minutes, which she accepted.

She turned her hand again to the problem of Chaim Uchida, who still had not made contact in response to her requests. She augmented her avatar's assertiveness quotient (to such a degree, in fact, that she became concerned it might convey as rude, but this was growing urgent), and navigated back towards the rail junction in anticipation. She grew aware, as she carried her small but increasingly heavy day-bag through the busy corridors of Woltjer's central district, that her neck-pain had resurfaced, though she decided against stopping to get a replacement derm-patch. She was in a hurry to return home.

It had just now occurred to her that Tanja's T-suit could not possibly have been a rental: it was embossed with a permanent name-patch. *Morgenstein.*

But if Tanja Morgenstein had never possessed a T-suit, then the suit most probably belonged to…

Yrsa Morgenstein.

At the time of her death, Tanja was wearing the T-suit she had borrowed from her mother.

Scarfe had no idea, at this point, what this meant. But it felt as though something, somewhere down the trajectory, might ultimately resolve itself from this.

She was generally averse to playing hunches, but she didn't have a lot else to work with right now. The sense she'd built up, from talking with Chavez and Kwan, and from the public-record info on her, was that Tanja Morgenstein had been a quiet, happily self-contained, self-assured young woman, hardly fitting the personality profile for those likely to end their own life in such a dramatic fashion, and without any explanatory justification. If there was any way in which the suit could somehow be material evidence of something untoward, then she needed to secure that suit, for further analysis. She forced herself to stop at a public bench, to sit and draft an urgent message to Kim N'Diaye, to ask Pathology to somehow hold the suit for a few more days.

The slate informed her that Chaim Uchida had finally responded to her repeated efforts at contact, and had nominated a meeting in approximately eighteen hours' time. She signalled "consent" before she'd had time to properly consider whether she could, in fact, get to Jeffreys fast enough to permit this appointment; but, somehow, she would find a way.

Sunder would need to mind their son for a third night: she was not going to be back in Trafton long enough for any Nikita-time to be more than merely disruptive. She still needed to touch base with her supervisor, Kalinda, but that must wait; she was in a hurry, now, to get to the rail terminus. *Leave it for the pod.*

The pod which she caught carried significantly more passengers than had the outbound one, though it was still hardly crowded; nonetheless, she felt her personal space intruded upon in a way it hadn't been earlier. She set the slate to arrange air travel from Trafton to Jeffreys (there was no rail connection to such a small settlement, and an overlander would take more time than she had available). Even so, it would be tight.

The slate reminded her that Jeffreys had an unenclosed air terminal, with no link-tubing. She'd be outside when she exited the flyer.

T-suit, then. As the rail-pod tugged itself into forward motion out of Woltjer East, she instructed the slate to make arrangements with her household servitor to ensure that her own suit was priority-consigned, as unaccompanied baggage, to meet her at Trafton air terminal. And she messaged Sunder about keeping Nikita for another night, not without conflicted emotions on her part. This done, she was out of admin tasks, and could justifiably sit back and enjoy the hesitant dawn that the rail-pod was now speeding towards... and yet the slow dissolve of darkness, ebbing to reveal a smearily-illuminated landscape of the rust-coloured ice plains that characterised eastern Xanadu, did not engage her enthusiasm as it normally would. Sleep would be useful: of the compartmentalised blocks of time from here, to Trafton, to Jeffreys for her meeting with Uchida, the rail-pod presented the longest interval within which to snatch sufficient hours of rest to ensure she arrived fresh and alert. But she was not, for the moment, tired: no, she was preoccupied with the as-yet-unanswered questions enveloping this case.

She might as well work. But the pod seemed busy enough that she did not feel able to review her existing interviews in a manner consistent with confidentiality requirements, so she scratched around for yet further background information, this time on Joshua Hainan and Yrsa Morgenstein, Tanja's parents.

There was considerably more on Hainan than on Morgenstein, naturally enough: industrialists outrank planetary geochemists. But as would have been expected for individuals of such prominence, what was publicly available nonetheless felt sanitised, as though Hainan, or perhaps some agency loyal to him, had been careful to airbrush the released material, so as to present the industrialist in an especially flattering light. This naturally had Scarfe wondering whether there was a hidden, darker side.

She asked the slate to arrange third-party-anonymised access to gripe sites mentioning either Hainan or his wife. Such information, she knew, would be intrinsically unreliable, but she wasn't intending to rely on these sites as a source of factual information, but rather as a rough guideline to the spread of public opinion regarding the couple.

Have to be careful not to get too coloured by this stuff, she told herself as the first such sites were identified for her. She began to read.

The slate beeped at her. *Nikita*, she thought, preparing her facial muscles for a smile, her throat for reassuring maternal warmth. But it wasn't Nikita, nor Sunder.

It was her supervisor.

Damn. I forgot. She had the slate extrude an earpiece and took the call, audio only. Her heart picked it up a notch. 'Kalinda?'

'Guerline. You've been a little hard to get hold of. Is everything alright?'

'It's fine,' she replied, purposefully avoiding the disapproving glance from a passenger, seated opposite, who was reading something off his own slate. 'It's a bit difficult to talk right now, I'm in transit.'

'So I hear. Guerline, we need to talk about the Tanja Morgenstein case.'

'What about it?' Scarfe asked, dry-mouthed and on the defensive already.

'There's a view – and it doesn't originate with me, but I can see the merit in it – that it may be prudent to backpedal somewhat. I'm sure you can understand that attention to this case is likely to cause considerable distress to her parents, who are already clearly suffering from the attention—'

'If you're implying that I've been unprofessional in my conduct on this one, I wish you'd just—'

'I'm not implying anything of the sort, Guerline.'

'Because I can assure you that I've approached this exactly as I would any other case.' She was finding it increasingly difficult to keep her resentment, her anger, concealed.

'I don't doubt that. But her parents are already the focus of considerable media attention as a result of this tragedy. Far more so than most parents.'

'You're asking me to shelve this, to, to *not investigate* the circumstances leading to Tan— to the client's death because of *the media*?' Slate-reader, opposite, raised his eyes to her again, held a glare. She cast her eyes down, breathed in, forced her voice to drop to a loud and impassioned whisper. 'Kalinda, this is contrary to every operating principle of the unit. We might as well just disband. Who's behind this?'

'I'm not saying anyone's behind this. I'm just saying there's merit in letting this lie. And you still have your auto-review summary to get to me, don't you?'

The auto-review. Shit. Her numbers hadn't been at all good this quarter. Nor last quarter. Too much time spent dotting and crossing. 'I still don't see why we'd be looking to circumvent standard practice just because the presenting family is...' *Wealthy. Powerful. Visibly dysfunctional.*

'It's not about who the family is, Guerline, it's about *not inflicting damage*. Promise me you'll get onto the auto-review business as a priority, okay?'

'I can do that,' she conceded. 'But I have one more interview scheduled for the Mor— for this one. One of the client's schoolfriends. It's taken quite an effort to get it set up, I'd like to see it through.'

'Then you'll let it rest?'

'I don't like leaving things unfinished.'

'Then write a report. *That's* how we finish things, Guerline. But prioritise the auto-review. Agreed?'

'Agreed,' she replied. And despised herself for the compliance. Kalinda always got under her skin exactly the way that Sunder used to; and her skin was – or should have been – her own territory.

'You're on your way back for this interview now?'

In a manner of speaking, Scarfe thought. 'Uh... yes.' *If Kalinda knew the interview was in Jeffreys, not just back in Trafton, would she still authorise it?*

She endured a couple of minutes of small talk, while striving not to incur the silent wrath of the passenger across the way. Found herself disclosing details of her relationship with her son which, in reality, Kalinda had no business knowing. She wished her supervisor goodbye and sat still for a couple of minutes while she centred herself. She wasn't sure why it was suddenly of higher importance to get to see Uchida, but it was.

And in the meantime, she couldn't work on her auto-review because one of the documents she needed for it was hardcopy only, on her desk. (And no time, on her Trafton stopover, to collect it.) *Such a shame.*

Why am I not just letting this go? I don't particularly identify with Tanja... is it that she'd lost her brother? Is it that I don't like being told to back off? Or is it that there's something about this scenario that just isn't right?

Questions are easy. Answers... answers can take a while, sometimes.

She returned her attention to the slate's gripe-site search results for Hainan and his wife.

By the time that she broke for a meal from the rail-pod's servomat, almost three hours later,she had learnt that the most common views aired concerning Joshua Hainan were that he was brash, single-minded, and ruthless. Of Yrsa Morgenstein there was considerably less written.

Armed with this impression of Hainan, she returned to the "approved" public record and perused it, to attempt to assess whether any of these perceptions might have a basis in reality.

On "brash", there was little to show one way or another. On "ruthless", though, there was quite a lot of evidence: claims of workplace victimisation; discrepancies in industrial safety record-keeping; cover-up allegations concerning fatal accidents at two of Hainan Global's brinemining facilities. While such complaints had always led to disciplinary action or termination of the conglomerate's middle-management staff rather than any of its leadership group, industry commentators wrote of a coercive corporate culture widely seen as reflective of Hainan's uncompromising aggressiveness.

Joshua Hainan, it seemed, was not a man to cross. Which meant, Scarfe thought, that she would need to tread carefully in Jeffreys, company town that it was.

five

She missed her pre-booked flight to Jeffreys. She was, in fact, close enough to be able to see it arc lazily into the orange-brown early-morning sky, right on schedule.

There'd been an obstacle on the rail. A big crawler-transporter, a Hainan Haulmaster, its articulated hoppers brimming with a load of hydrocarbon sand from the southwest Fensal dunes, had broken down on the rail crossing just beyond the Trafton settlement limits. So she watched in impotence from the nearest lay-by, her view partially obscured by a large stained-ice cairn, as a T-suited work gang struggled to rectify the problem. They'd evidently been at it for some time: her rail-pod was fourth in the lay-by queue. She swore inwardly at the delay. Others in the rail-pod were less private with their condemnation: two young men, in particular, were so strident in their statements that she became concerned a brawl might actually develop, as other passengers sought to rebuke them over their aggression.

It was a relief, on several levels, when the first of the waiting rail-pods was finally able to proceed, and fifteen minutes later their own vehicle was once again in motion. But the pod was running three hours late.

She placed another avatar-call to Uchida, requesting a three-hour delay on their meeting due to "circumstances beyond my control", and signalled "Send". It was too much to hope, of course, that he'd actually respond: she had mentally already placed Chaim Uchida in a box labelled "difficult to get hold of". But she had at least made the appropriate effort.

Disembarking at the Trafton rail junction, she manifested what, for her, was an unaccustomed display of physical assertiveness as she manoeuvred her way ahead of others exiting the vehicle, and then through the noisy crowd that almost filled the junction concourse. It was with some small feeling of personal satisfaction that she succeeded in nosing in front of the two particularly vocal young men from the pod. Her sensation of an insignificant victory was blunted, however, when she realised that, in her haste, she had left her day-bag on the pod's seating. She slowed, unexpectedly enough that she was jostled from behind, and for a few moments she contemplated going back. But retracing her steps, now, would add a further ten-minute delay, and without this she still had a slim prospect of getting to Jeffreys on time. And she had on her the most important items: her slate and her ID. So, still on the move, she placed a message with the station's "Lost Items" service, identifying herself, her luggage, confirming that it contained no proscribed items (though, of course, the station staff could scan as much for themselves), and authorising credit for its return to her residence.

She was nonetheless angry at herself for this lapse. Why was she allowing the Morgenstein case to so preoccupy her that she was now failing at routine tasks?

Because there is something about it which just does not add up. Tanja Morgenstein had provided no reason for—

60

Worry about this later. Worry about it once you've dropped the case, because Kalinda asked you to drop it. Right now your priority is finding a way to get to Jeffreys on time.

It was thanks to the slate that she already knew, on her arrival at Trafton Airstation's unaccompanied-baggage counter, that there were no further scheduled flights to Jeffreys within the next ten hours. Which meant she'd need to resort to a rental.

She signed for her T-suit case and wheeled it across the concourse, asking the slate to sort through the available rental options for her. Quickest, it transpired, would be an airhopper. Her heart sank at the cost, but she really didn't have a choice: there was nothing else available which stood any chance of getting her to her meeting with Uchida. She asked the slate to invest five minutes in seeking anyone who might be willing to share the expense with her, but wasn't really surprised that, given the exceptionally short notice, there were no takers. *Finance is not going to be happy. Nor is Kalinda.* But given the difficulties she'd had arranging this appointment with the elusive Uchida, she judged it was this, or nothing. (Or rather, the less-preferred option of a virt session; but she knew that the meeting with Chavez and Kwan would not have been so informative at such a remove. There were some things you only got by sitting in a room with someone.)

On *that* front... 'Current or last known location, if public, of Joshua Hainan?' she asked the slate.

<Joshua Hainan is flagged as at large in Jeffreys,> replied the slate.

Great, she thought. *So this really is into the lion's den.* Not that she was doing anything unauthorised, but she was being persistent;

and she was aware that this might well come across to a man like Hainan as intrusiveness. Even if Scarfe's stated goal was to obtain background information, if possible, on the reasons underpinning Tanja Morgenstein's tragic decision.

'And Yrsa Morgenstein?'

<Yrsa Morgenstein's whereabouts aren't currently a matter of public record.>

What, really, was she hoping to achieve through this meeting with Uchida? She didn't know. She knew that there were pieces missing, but whether Uchida could or would supply them to her was a matter of misty conjecture. Still, if she didn't pursue this, she'd always be left wondering. *Stones are not for leaving unturned. Not in this game.*

And yet Kalinda wants—

She instructed the slate to set up the airhopper rental for her, and headed for a vacant change-lock.

<Do you need to be updated on your messages, Guerline?> her T-suit asked, as she paced carefully across the groomed-ice surface towards the sleek shape of the waiting airhopper.

'No,' she replied, self-conscious of the amplified, reverberative sound of her breathing, and of her own voice. It didn't help that the suit still had that characteristic smell of long disuse. *I really should get outside more. But where to find the time?*

<Do you wish to establish a music programme for your journey today?>

'No.'

<Can I arrange anything by way of entertainment for you?>

'No. Thank you.' *I checked my slate not ten minutes ago. Can't the suit appreciate that I might like a little downtime, a bit of silence?*

But of course, it was an old model, she'd had it six years—not as old as the suit Tanja died in, but nowhere near as high-end either. Her own suit's intellect was... probably the most charitable term would be "rudimentary".

The Hainan Peoplelifter was a wide-winged six engine five-seater with VTOL capability and an airlock too cramped to allow her to even remove her helmet. She climbed aboard and gave the airlock pumps and sprays a minute to remove the worst of her suit's Titan-stink. Once through into the cabin proper, she strapped herself into the front seat and inspected the display in front of her. The controls were extremely basic, as befitted a craft fully capable of flying itself.

It'd better be, she noted acerbically, inspecting the pudgy fingers of her T-suit's glove. *I sure as hell couldn't.* She selected "Jeffreys" from among the pre-loaded destinations, and punched "Go".

The Peoplelifter gave an unsettling shake, started to hum at increasing pitch—something she as much felt as heard through her suit—and pulled itself ponderously into the sky. Then, once it had reached five thousand metres, it commenced lateral motion. She unlatched her helmet, winced at the residual odour, pulled off still-chilled gloves.

Jeffreys was north-north-east of Trafton, a thousand kilometres plus change. The journey would take about four and a half hours. She could see, ahead, the start of the Fensal dune-belt proper: dark-ochre parallel lines, nearly perfectly straight, interspersed with the even darker shadows of the long valleys between the ridges of hydrocarbon sand. To her right, what she initially took to be some light-coloured smear on the outside of the Peoplelifter's viewport was, she eventually decided, the slow-rising sun, struggling, this early in the week-long Titanian day, to punch its way through the thick, messy atmosphere.

Of crescent Saturn, which would lie somewhat higher than the Sun in the sky, there was no discernible sign.

Another time, she'd have watched the unfolding landscape, but today she was not in the mood. There was too much jumble in her head: the deepening enigma of Tanja's demise; a sense of brooding unease at the prospect that Finance might not sign off on reimbursement of this admittedly costly jaunt to Jeffreys; plus the comedown from the adrenaline rush she had been on for the past several hours since the rail-pod's delay in getting back into Trafton. She was increasingly aware that her sleep cycle had been thrown out. *Have to tend to that once I've done with Uchida,* she told herself. The problem, though, was that her eyelids were growing heavy *now…*

She came to with a start, disturbed by some barely-perceptible change in the Peoplelifter's attitude: there was evidently a bit of a crosswind at this altitude, not strong but erratic. Disoriented, she asked the craft for the time elapsed since takeoff, and was disheartened to be told that it was less than half an hour. *Still another four to go.* And she knew that however fatigued she felt, she wouldn't manage to settle back into sleep again. But she was feeling too muzzy, for now, for the idea of thinking over the case to be appealing.

She reached for her helmet. 'Suit? What were those entertainment possibilities you mentioned?'

The suit, she suspected, would have preferred to continue offering her distractions, but the sporadic turbulence wasn't conducive to immersion in *Sagan Crisis Team 5*, and the visor's aging electronics struggled to present clean crisp images in true-D. It felt, she thought, like watching surveillicam footage through green mud. She disengaged after the game's second mission, removing her helmet once again, hoping she hadn't inflicted a tension headache upon herself. *Still over an hour to go.*

The cabin did not seem to have warmed any.

She put the helmet back on. 'Don't get excited,' she told the suit. 'I'm not up for another instalment of *SCT5*—I just need you to display some images for me. Yrsa Morgenstein's graduation. I've viewed them previously, within the past three days.'

<It would be a pleasure, Guerline. Are these the ones you mean?> A mosaic of thumbnails manifested itself on the visor's viewscreen.

'Yes, that's them. Can you fullscreen the middle image from the lower row for me?'

<Middle left or middle right?> asked the suit.

'Left.' *Now, allowing for the vagaries of the visor's colour palette…* 'Is there any way you can bring that into the correct colours for me?'

<Guerline,> replied the suit, with what she could swear was a tone of reproach, *<those colours* are *the correct colours.>*

They're so not, she thought, but did not argue further.

Whatever the image's deficiencies of tone, it showed a woman clad in a close-fitting dark grey suit with varicoloured, brocaded blouse, adorned with a delicate necklace and a large jewelled brooch. Her hair, gripped aloft in a bun, took on the semblance of a handle atop her head, and her hand, sporting three rings, lightly held a furled roll of paper or plastic. The woman's smile was serious, composed, victorious, and her stance, though relaxed, looked far from spontaneous. *It's not so much a picture,* Scarfe thought, *as a portrait: something taken for posterity.*

The woman could very well have been Tanja Morgenstein, captured in life just a few short daycycles ago, in an outfit she left lying in a stowbank locker; but it wasn't. The image dated from almost fifty years ago, decades before Tanja's birth.

Yrsa Morgenstein had been over thirty years old at the time. Guerline puzzled over that—she hadn't had need, before this, to quantify the ages of Tanja's parents, it wasn't a direct consideration in the case. They were still fit, still retained vigour, thanks no doubt to a carefully-maintained course of youth-extending treatments… but wasn't leaving it until sixty rather late to be having children? On a physical level, aside from any other considerations? The rejuvenants weren't of much benefit in prolonging fertility.

According to the available information, Joshua Hainan and Yrsa Morgenstein had been together for almost three decades before they had started a family. Which was… odd. And difficult to comprehend.

What changed, after three decades?

She'd called up this portrait to check the outfit, not to puzzle over chronological details of the Hainan-Morgenstein family history. And the outfit matched.

The clothes in the image appeared to be the very same items as those that still sat in the locker. Including, in all probability, the shoes. Which implied—what?

What does it mean, Scarfe wondered, *that Tanja apparently contemplated wearing an outfit of symbolic value to her mother, an outfit tied in closely with her mother's identity, for her final fatal excursion? What caused her change of heart?*

And the hairstyle, the jewellery, her mother's suit—there's a definite message there.

I think Runag Fischetti must have heard it correctly: Tanja did mention a note, and "she" can only mean her mother. But did Yrsa Morgenstein get the note ... and if so, what did it say?

Height, the smoky shadows of still-early morning, and a badly-fogged viewscreen all conspired to hinder Scarfe's appraisal of the terrain towards which the Peoplelifter, still battling the crosswind, was slowly descending. Lines of umber-tinted dunes that had appeared to be merely pencil-thin ultimately revealed themselves to be hundreds of metres wide. A distant, barely-darker ovoid blotch, sepia-rimmed, looming some indeterminate distance ahead to the northwest, finally resolved itself into the crater Momoy, a rugged basin easily large enough to swallow all of sprawling Sagan, should it have so wished. But the settlement of Jeffreys, hunched beside that crater amidst the wide-strewn dunes that stretched all the way east to the horizon and beyond, refused to make full geometric sense until she was very nearly on top of it.

It was on pylons. The whole blocky, modular conglomeration of the habitat—even, it seemed, the broad airpad that skirted its south-eastern aspect—was raised on thick tubular pylons, lifting the settlement ten, fifteen, twenty metres above the undulating and rutted terrain of the dunebed. Was this, she wondered, for heat-engineering purposes, as was done with the "floating" hotels of Ligeia, to minimise contact with the sea's supercold liquid? Or was it some form of defence against western Fensal's slow-drifting dunes?

Scarfe had more important matters to attend to; she wasn't sufficiently curious to consider the question further. But she did know, as the Peoplelifter shuddered and droned in its final, bumpy climb-down, that she didn't feel entirely comfortable about landing on a surface that was still a probably-lethal height above the world's deep-frozen surface.

She couldn't decide whether to be angry, or concerned, or an amalgam of both: Chaim Uchida had been a no-show at the appointment she had gone to so much trouble and expense to make. She waited in the Jeffreys common area for ten minutes, fifteen, twenty: no sign. And no acknowledgement of her most recent messages. *I give up rostered time with my son, and you don't even make the meeting?* Anger won over concern, now that she sat with it. She checked the time: it was well outside his designated hours of active employment. *No excuse, then.*

'Current or last publicly-known location of Chaim Uchida?' she asked the slate.

<Chaim Uchida's whereabouts aren't currently a matter of public record.>
Great. 'Location of Uchida's private residence?'

<Chaim Uchida's personal habitation is listed as level three, unit 385A. Please note, however, that—>

'I know, present whereabouts unknown,' she interrupted. 'I *got* that. Just guide me there, okay?'

Chaim Uchida was a mess. His small apartment was hardly better.

Professional, she warned herself. Scarfe started with a begrudging apology for intruding on him.

'No, you made the appointment,' he said, beckoning for her to follow him into the barely-lit depths of his living-space. 'I should have kept it, you've come some distance. I just...' He left unstated whatever further explanation might have existed, gestured instead for the investigator to be seated on a solid-polymer chair. 'Is it alright if we do it here?'

Scarfe mapped out the room—strewn with perhaps a week's worth of flotsam: discarded meal wrappings and utensils, clothing of uncertain laundry status, and miscellaneous flimsies—and Uchida himself, wearing a long tunic with all-too-evident food stains, and sporting the reddest-rimmed eyes Scarfe had seen in several months. *He's in no fit state to be out in public, looking as he does. Nor does he present any threat,* she thought. *Except maybe to himself.* 'Yes, here is fine,' she said, in what she hoped was a tone of reassurance: something, she sensed, that Uchida needed a lot of right now. 'I normally make a point of recording these sessions—I'm officially obligated to do that, though of course the records aren't retained indefinitely,' she explained. 'But if you'd prefer, we can do this off-the-record.'

'No,' he said. 'No, I'd rather this be done properly. If you normally make a record, then let's do that. Please.'

'Thank you,' she said, and brought out the recorder. She placed it carefully among the chaos of the meal table in front of her. 'I appreciate that the subject we're going to touch on today could well be upsetting for you. Please let me know if, at any time, you need a break from the dialogue.'

'I think I'd just rather get it done,' he said. 'If that's all the same to you.'

'Thanks,' she said. *May as well start at the deep end then.* 'Can you tell me, please, what was Tanja like?'

Seated across the table from her, Chaim Uchida dissolved into tears.

It was a long discussion, and at first frequently interrupted, as Uchida gave himself up repeatedly to the intensity of his grief. The professional side of Scarfe surmised, at first, that it had been a mistake to press for this meeting: this young man seemed too bereft, too innately distraught, for anything constructive to happen here, while her human side felt an almost unbearably awkward guilt in the presence of his evident pain.

She was accustomed to grief, of course, as displayed by parents, lovers, spouses, sometimes just apparently distant friends—and on a personal level, she had felt, herself, its cold, embrittling embrace—but the strength of Uchida's emotion was something she did not often see. It was hard not to feel voyeuristic, even ghoulish, at allowing the dialogue to continue. But Uchida insisted. And like a tipped bottle, like his abiding sense of loss, once his words were unstoppered they could not be contained.

After the first half hour, his upset grew less extreme, less prone to leaving him overwhelmed. After an hour, she sensed that Uchida was largely relieved at having found someone to whom he could talk about this. After one-and-a-half hours, Guerline Scarfe was wondering whether anybody before this, even Tanja herself, had ever fully comprehended the strength of his feelings towards Tanja Morgenstein.

It's not healthy, she thought, *to lose oneself so deeply in another. Not healthy at all. But it does happen.*

By this stage. she had a sense of Tanja that was so strong—for all that it may have been so partial as to be utterly one-sided—that she felt she knew the woman well enough to grieve her herself. But the clincher came at the two-hour-and-twenty-minute mark, when Uchida had moved onto the topic—and now she truly did feel uncomfortably voyeuristic—of physical intimacy.

'We were always very careful,' he explained. 'Because of who she was, and what a big deal, a big bad deal, it would be if anything was to happen. Not just with interpersonal hygiene, I mean, also in terms of... starting something.'

'You mean pregnancy?'

He nodded. 'Which was silly, I guess—or just overcautious— because she'd been fairly certain for a few years that she was infertile. She thought it was hereditary.'

'How,' asked Scarfe, guardedly, 'can infertility be hereditary?'

'She wasn't sure of the specifics. I think she tried talking to her mother about it once, but I don't think that got her anywhere useful. Yrsa Morgenstein isn't the easiest person to talk to. Particularly about stuff like that.'

I can well imagine. But Scarfe kept the words to herself. 'What made her think her infertility was genetic?'

'There was something Yrs—her mother said, that they tried for decades before they made Piotr.'

'They said made? Not conceived?'

'That was what Tanja said. I think. They did talk odd sometimes.'

'Can I ask if you know why Tanja was concerned with this? To ask her mother, I mean? Twenty's not... uh, were you planning...'

'Not really, not yet, no. She just wanted to know what was up with her body.'

'What do you mean, what was up with her body?'

71

'I honestly don't know, she didn't tell me what she was worried about. She had insecurities, which I think her parents encouraged. They were very controlling, I thought. Yrsa especially. Hainan wasn't around that much—he was mainly here in Jeffreys.'

'How did it work, with you in Jeffreys and Tanja in Trafton?'

'It wasn't ideal. I got to see her for a couple of days every fortnight. I tried making it longer sometimes, but the shifts never worked out somehow.' A scowl brushed across Uchida's face. 'Hainan.'

'So this was you travelling to Trafton? Or did Tanja ever come here?'

Uchida glanced about the room, its chaos and grubbiness. 'No. There was never any question of that. I asked sometimes, but it was just never possible. Her parents.'

Like a princess in a tower, Scarfe thought.

Uchida talked on with hardly any prompting, but there was little more of apparent significance. Scarfe, sensing that her blood-sugar levels were getting dangerously low, finally capped the interview off at three-plus hours.

'Thank you for making yourself available,' she said, awkwardly standing to leave. She'd thoroughly outworn the solid chair's welcome. 'Please don't hesitate to contact me if any of this gets too much.' (Translation: *don't do anything rash.*) She offered her hand to shake, something she had quite neglected to do at the interview's onset.

'Thank *you*,' he replied. His grip was polite, brief, a little hot.

'How do you want to arrange the transcript?'

'I don't need a transcript. It's in here,' he said, rapping his chest.

'My directives are that I should—'

'Please,' he said. 'I'd just rather not.' And his mouth wavered before it closed, while his eyes took on a distant, lost look, directed straight at Scarfe but plainly not seeing her.

'Are you sure—' she began.

'There was something,' he said, speaking hurriedly, as though afraid he would lose his nerve if he slowed. 'The last couple of days, before she, before she… she wasn't right. And she wouldn't say why. She wasn't saying anything.' He sat down again, would not look at Scarfe.

She waited, concerned, hungry, perhaps even a little light-headed, to see if there was more, but there wasn't. Against her better judgement, she sat down facing him once more. 'What do you mean, she wasn't right?' She was annoyed, because this possible-revelation was at variance with Uchida's earlier assurance that there had been no problems of any significance in his relationship with Tanja. She also suspected him of having engineered a situation in which it would be too intrusive to restart the recorder. 'Had something happened between you two?'

'No, it… I mean, I don't think so. I mean, I don't recall that we'd argued or anything. But we were just, for that time, there was something… something she wouldn't say. And she didn't want to see me. Didn't even want to take my calls. That really hurt. She means, she meant so…' And he stopped. He had run dry, he'd lost his nerve. She could read it on his face.

'Chaim,' said Guerline, with all the patience she could muster. '*What happened* those last couple of days, between you and Tanja?'

'Nothing happened,' he explained. 'Or something happened, I mean that's obvious, because she wasn't, she wasn't herself, but I've honestly no idea what it was. She just wasn't talking, and that scared me, because we always talked. She said she just needed to be by herself for a bit. And that was the last thing, I think the last thing she said to me, before she—'

'Chaim,' she said to him, resisting an impulse to reach her hand across to his arm, 'I understand that this is causing you considerable anguish.' *The fact you've kept it bottled up throughout three hours of conversation is testament to that.* 'But you can't let these what-ifs prey at you. The past can't be changed; and the present must be lived. You mustn't hold yourself responsible for not predicting a tragedy. These concerns you have, these doubts, they're not uncommon in situations such as this.' Which was true enough, but there was still something about Uchida's latest muddled utterances that niggled at her. It was obvious, from what he had said, that something had been building up within Tanja Morgenstein; but it was clear, also, that the person for Guerline to put such thoughts to was not Uchida, not now. 'Seriously, I would recommend grief counselling. I think it would help you to work such issues through.'

'Thank you,' he replied. 'I will.'

She suspected he wouldn't. But she'd made the suggestion.

She took her leave.

six

Making her way to the habitat's elevator, she stopped at an autovendor for a bulb of culturebroth, which she sipped as her slate guided her back towards the airstation. The moods of her interview with Uchida orbited awkwardly within her mind, like nebulous planets within some dimly-lit orrery. She fumbled for a sense of something more defined, more tangible: what happened between Uchida and Tanja in those last couple of days of her life? Or, at least, what crisis did Tanja experience?

She was missing something. She'd known that from the outset.

The corridors were reasonably busy – it appeared to be the changeover for one of the standard shifts – and she was twice jostled by people as she walked. Then, having turned the corner, she was met by a larger group, a dense enough knot of people that they quite blocked the narrow passageway. They did not make way for her at all; she was forced to stand her ground while they moved past, like a chill methane stream bifurcating at an ice outcrop. One of them, ostensibly looking to move out of the way of someone behind him, actually walked straight into her. She saved herself from falling, but the culturebroth bulb, only half-spent, went flying. It impacted on someone at the back of the group, spilling a substantial amount on the man's dark business uniform.

She stepped aside, seeking the wall's relative safety. 'I do apologise,' she began to say—

—and a hand latched onto her upper arm. A strong hand, a youthful hand, applied with sufficient force that it was sure to leave bruises. It surprised her, even in the moment, that she didn't drop the slate. She raised her eyes, flaring angrily, to meet her accoster.

Joshua Hainan.

She stared into his weathered face, flicked her glance down accusingly at his arm; he released his hold. She let her gaze fall lower, to the hand that hung from his sleeve like a weapon; he slid the offending hand behind his back. She pointedly raised her eyes again to meet his.

'Be with you soon,' he boomed out, a long-distance voice: not for her benefit, but that of the receding group.

The man and the woman who flanked him, also now stopped, were so bulky and stern in appearance that she could not help but classify them as bodyguards. Guerline looked to find a path through between them, but they might as well have formed a wall.

'I am most sincerely sorry,' she said, struggling to meet his stern gaze. Hainan was probably the person she least wished to see at this moment. 'But if you don't mind, I am in quite—'

'I don't wish to detain you,' he said, while seeking to blot up as much of his suit's broth decoration as could be absorbed by the formerly-neatly-pressed handkerchief in his hand. 'But what brings you all the way to Jeffreys?'

Her heartbeat had gone up a level, but she forced her voice to remain flat, unhurried, professional. 'I was visiting a client.'

'Of course. I was wanting to talk with you about Tan— about your investigation. I don't believe it's in anyone's best interests.'

'There is a process,' said Scarfe, with careful emphasis, 'which I am compelled by law to follow.' Some unformed thought was nagging at her, something important…

He was not to be deflected. He had ten centimetres on her, more, plus that bulk. 'Have you ever lost a child of your own?' he asked.

Her thoughts flew immediately to Nikita, so small, so trusting, so vulnerable. Then to her brother. 'No. No, not a child. But I—'

'Then you know nothing of this. You're causing my family considerable distress. It needs to stop.' He tilted his head, directly meeting her gaze. His eyes narrowed. 'You need to make it stop.'

'Mr Hainan,' she replied. 'I sympathise with your personal pain, the anguish you and your… family must be experiencing. But my duties are to explore the reasons why such… tragic incidents like Tanja's occur, to determine if there are ways in which Fensal could be better safeguarding its citizens. I have to believe that's a worthwhile goal, no matter the anguish that might result from the process.'

A recycling trundler was making its way past them, along the corridor; Hainan offhandedly dropped the soiled handkerchief into its maw. The pair of bodyguards wordlessly repositioned themselves in the trundler's wake so as, it seemed, to better block her escape.

'I don't care,' he told her, in words that were measured out like a dose, 'what you believe. I don't care what might happen in the future, to anybody else. I have no interest in improving things for some nebulous "others". I insist that this investigation into *my* daughter's suicide, which is right now causing *my* family real pain, must be suspended.' He lifted his hand to his neck, in what at first she mistook for a throat-slitting signal; but it was the finger-down-the-collar gesture that she remembered from the interview. Scratchy shirt?

'There is a procedure,' she replied with forced false calm, striving to keep her gaze raised above his neck, 'that must be followed. I am following it.' She exhaled heavily, tried to draw herself up. 'Now I really must be returning to Trafton. Please excuse me.' She took a step across, looking to pass between Hainan and the female bodyguard. For a second she was convinced that he was going to reach out and accost her again, but he evidently thought better of the gesture and lowered his hand. The bodyguard moved just enough that Guerline could squeeze past.

She felt Hainan's eyes on her back all the way to the corridor's next bend; it took longer than that for the adrenaline to ebb. Longer still the sense of humiliation.

It was true, as Hainan had intimated, that she had never herself directly experienced the pain of a parent losing a child. But she had known other losses, she'd seen that pain, written plain as a map, on the faces of a good many other parents, she had heard their torment in the words they'd struggled to assemble, she had tasted their all-too-apparent despair. She had never seen anyone react towards her – in her professional capacity, at least – with even half the hostility that Hainan had just now exhibited. Grief, she knew, could make people do strange things, but was grief truly Hainan's wellspring, or was this something else?

Should she stop probing? What good could come of it?

But you have a duty. You've done nothing wrong. You're merely fulfilling your responsibilities.

Every few steps, there was another question.

What could cause the daughter of an aggressive, domineering businessman to contemplate, much less to commit, such a desperate act?

What is it that underpins Yrsa Morgenstein's unconcealed animosity towards her husband?

What did Tanja put in the note to her mother? And, since it hasn't been found, where did she hide that note?

Let it go, Gwer. Like Kalinda wants you to. Like Hainan wants you to.

But she knew she wouldn't.

The slate informed her that the next scheduled flight to Trafton was over seven hours away. She registered for it, resigning herself to a long wait in the uninspiring environment of the airstation lounge, and made her way to the station storage lockers. As she went to lift her suit-bag out, she suddenly went rigid, caught an awkward breath, and her surroundings ceased, momentarily, to make any sense to her.

Oh. Oh, shit. Yes, it could, couldn't it?

She straightened up, holding the bag, simultaneously feeling flushed and chilled.

Navigating through a lounge suddenly filled with the tinnitus of disorientation, she found a vacant bench, got her slate out again, and bade it arrange an airhopper back to Trafton, as soon as possible. Then she instructed the slate, in the formal terms necessary for such a step, to encrypt, as "Personal – Only", all record of the interview she had conducted with Chaim Uchida.

<Guerline, are you sure about this?>

No, of course I'm not sure. But I can say he didn't want it recorded. And I don't wish this to be accessible to Kalinda, unless I decide it appropriate.
'Yes. Do it. Now.'

And now you can't say any more that you've done nothing wrong. But it's about to get worse.

There were airhoppers available, so there was no point in delaying. She picked up the bulky suit-bag and crossed to the bank of personal airlocks.

seven

The vehicle this time, her suit informed her, was a Volker Skyrider, a sleek one-person, eight-engine craft with batteryprop-terminated wings fore and aft; this model was apparently a civilian adaptation of a mil surveillance / combat craft. It was not a vehicle Scarfe had flown before, and she was somewhat disconcerted to learn that the "cockpit", as such, consisted merely of a C-fibre seatframe with a septum-seal data umbilical for interfacing with the occupant's suit. The seat was not even fully enclosed; the occupant-access opening in the top of the fuselage was protected at the front and sides by a wraparound screen. It dawned on Scarfe that the top of her T-suit helmet would in fact form part of the vehicle's streamlining: it wasn't a thought to engender confidence. Still, the suit assured her that, freed from the dual encumbrances of an airlock and a hermetically-sealed cabin, the Skyriders were reasonably *fast*.

Fast was good.

She climbed in awkwardly, sat: even through her T-suit's padded insulation, she could feel the seat's ice-hard chill. There was a whirr down to her right, as the data umbilical mated with her suit's flank. She was just about to complain – to the suit, because there was nobody else here – that there were no controls visible, when the Heads-Up Display on her helmet's visor revealed a pre-flight safety message.

The engines powered up. A young-sounding male voice, not her suit's voice, asked her to where she wished to fly.

'So does my preferred operating temperature actually *mean* anything?' she asked, over the low roar of the props and the rush of wind against her helmet. 'Or is it just some kind of thermal placebo?'

<*My apologies, Guerline,*> intoned the suit. <*I appear to have overcompensated for the ambient. Calibrating now.*>

Five minutes in the air, and she was baking. Perspiration rolled down her face, stung eyes she could not wipe.

It was a small craft, and the wind was capricious. The flight was reasonably turbulent, with a disturbing degree of sashay and some alarming momentary dips in altitude. She had opted for the most direct route, cutting straight over the dunefields of western Fensal (not that she could actually see them from here, unless she wished to choose that option from the inflight HUD). The Skyrider had advised that an arced flightpath, skirting the dunefields, might also avoid the turbulence, but she didn't feel inclined to divert for a "might". This route would get her home in under three hours.

She waited until she had been airborne for fifteen minutes or so before she had her T-suit flag a call to Kim N'Diaye. It was a few minutes more before he answered, and the transmission was patchy.

'Guerline?' he asked, loud, hesitant. 'There's a lot of background noise.'

'There would be,' she yelled back to him. 'I'm in flight right now, heading back from Jeffreys in, apparently, a streamlined echo chamber.'

'Ah. Right. To what do I— what can I do for you?'

'Do you still have the Morgenstein T-suit?'

'Yes,' he replied. 'Has Yrsa M been on your back about it too?'

'What? No… no. But I need to get access to it.' She managed to keep her tone steady as the plane took an utterly unforeshadowed dip of several metres, followed by a lurch to the left. It occurred to her, as the vehicle shuddered alarmingly, that she hadn't seen any mention of a parachute among the aircraft's inventory.

'Access?' N'Diaye asked.

'I need to retrieve something from it. You need to promise you won't release that suit, under any circumstances, to Tanja's parents. Not yet, not until I've had time to—'

'Guerline.' That deep sing-song voice, thick with paternalistic concern. 'What is this about?'

'It's… look, it's better that I explain in person.' *Ideally once I've managed to turn this over a bit more in my mind. There's still stuff I'm missing.* 'But it's imperative that that suit stay in Pathology's possession until I've had a chance to inspect it.'

'Inspect it? We've already been over it, the suit was fully functional. There are— there were no mechanical issues with it whatsoever. My team was utterly thorough.'

She could well believe that, given N'Diaye's history. If there was anyone who would take particular care over possible faults in a T-suit, that person would be Kim N'Diaye, still not fully in command of his prosthetic legs. 'It's *not a mechanical issue.*'

'Then what—'

'Just, please, hold it for me.' An unsettling thought occurred to her. 'You… you haven't released the body, I presume?' *I hope?*

'No, but we were looking to hand—'

'Don't. There are far too many unanswered questions on this case. Tanja Morgenstein's body could yet be evidence of something.' *Well-adjusted twenty-year-old females – and despite all of the baggage of her upbringing and her identity, I'm convinced that Tanja would best be described as "well-adjusted" – just do not commit suicide on a whim. There is something really troubling here, and that suit could hold the secret.*

'What do I tell Yrsa M if she puts the pressure on again?'

'Just tell her you're running more tests. That's true enough. Or if that's not enough – I don't know, Kim, tell her anything. Lie if you have to.'

'*Lie* if I have to? To Joshua Hainan's partner?'

'Yes. If that's what it takes.'

'I have to say, Guerline, I hope you've got a really good explanation for all of this…'

I hope so too. 'I have.'

The plane initiated a slow bank to the left. She was rewarded, if "rewarded" was the right word, with a sighting of the striated brown-and-black tableau of the dunefields, stretching like a road – like a sea – like a limitless band of dark, ridged cloth, all the way to the eastern horizon. Still low above that horizon, the sun was no more than a feeble blemish, a small half-light defect in the rust-washed sky, while above, the hesitant, nebulous watermark of Saturn – at this time of day, almost new, though still palely ring-winged – loomed like an omen.

<Passenger Scarfe,> the aircraft's voice intoned within her helmet. *<There is a difficulty.>*

'What do you mean, "difficulty"?'

The suit chimed in. *<Guerline, we don't have sufficient reserves of power to reach Trafton. We must attempt to return to Jeffreys.>*

'What? Why?'

<Insufficient reserves of motive power exist to—>

'I got *that* part,' she snapped. The aircraft was still veering left; and, now that she was paying attention to such matters, was descending slowly, though still at an altitude of several kilometres. A quick check of the HUD confirmed that she was significantly less than an hour into a three-hour flight. No longer merely inconvenient, the size of the dunefield was now something ominous. Beckoning. 'I missed the part about *how* this plane is short of charge. Wasn't it completely recharged at Jeffreys?'

<Passenger Scarfe. I can confirm that the vessel diagnosed as ready-to-fly at our outset. However, a fault has developed with Battery Cluster Two, which is not delivering current. It is probable that the cluster itself remains functional, but the connection is impaired to the point of failure.>

She forced herself to sound measured, rational, while her heart rate climbed. She grew suddenly sensitive to every modulation of the engines' multi-throated droning, every minuscule shudder. 'Can you not diagnose and rectify inflight?'

<Guerline, this is a return-to-base fault. We must attempt to return to Jeffreys.>

'What do you mean, attempt?'

<It is not clear that accessible reserves will be sufficient for task.>

'So we're just going to *ditch*?'

<That is the safest course of action in the circumstances. Emergency crews at Jeffreys have been notified. A descent close to the settlement will minimise the time for crews to reach you.>

That's not all it'll do. It'll delay my access to the Morgenstein T-suit. And N'Diaye won't be able to stonewall indefinitely against Yrsa's demands for its return. An ember of anger kindled in her. Kalinda's pressure to drop the matter. The obstacle on the rail-pod track, just out of Trafton. The run-in with Hainan, and his clear attempt to bully her into compliance. And now *this*. 'Go around,' she ordered, while blinking down the gain on her HUD to reduce the glare from the bright beige smudge of the sun, now directly ahead of her in the browned-orange sky. 'Maintain original course.'

<Guerline, the aircraft doesn't have sufficient charge to reach your intended destination. We must endeavour to return to Jeffreys. Do you not comprehend this?>

'I comprehend, all right,' Scarfe responded. 'But provided we get more than halfway before we ditch, it'll be the Trafton crews that come for us.' *That maintenance worker at the airstation. Or am I being paranoid, seeing conspiracy where ill-chance might be the culprit?* But she knew whose purpose was served by a delay, and it certainly wasn't hers. And a return to Jeffreys was undoubtedly a delay, whether by accident… or design.

<It is not clear that the charge is sufficient to reach a halfway point. In any event, Passenger Scarfe, a forward course will not get us clear of the dunefields. I cannot land in the dunefields. We must return to Jeffreys.>

She put as much steel as possible into her voice. 'I gave you a direct order. Hold to original course. Comply. And notify the emergency crews at Trafton.'

The aircraft straightened out, steadied. It banked incrementally to the right.

<Guerline, this is highly inadvisable. As a construct charged with maintaining your wellbeing, I must protest.>

'Noted,' she replied, musing on the suit's choice of words. 'It's just the *vehicle* short of power, isn't it? Can this umbilical carry charge?'

How much charge, she wondered, *does it take to keep a low-mass airframe in the air for three hours?*

A T-suit is, by law, required to carry charge sufficient to maintain four standard days' life support for its inhabitant, under "wilderness conditions"…

<Affirmative, Guerline.>

'That's a "yes" to which question?'

<To both of them.>

'Right. Then find a power-distribution strategy that has this flight terminating in Trafton, as intended.'

<Guerline, it isn't just a matter of total power consumption.> The suit, she thought, sounded… pained. <It's a matter of rate of consumption. My power-storage systems aren't designed for such high throughput to both power the aircraft and maintain internal warmth.>

'Then ease back on the environment conditioning,' she instructed. 'Is that… doable?'

<From a purely technical perspective, yes.> "Pained", she now thought, wasn't sufficiently strong a word. <However, I have grave concerns over such a course of action.>

'Get me to Trafton,' she said. 'I don't care if I'm chilled to the bone, as long as I'm alive and conscious. Is there a power-distribution strategy that permits that?'

There was an alarmingly long pause.

<This instruction cuts across all of my programming.>

'Answer the question. Is there a power-distribution strategy that deprioritises environment conditioning, keeps me conscious, and still gets this flight to Trafton?'

<There is. But, Guerline—>

'Do it. Now. That is an order.'

Scarfe shook, and not just from the cold. The rational part of her mind was slick with fear.

The suit had had the Skyrider climb steadily, a gradual but unnervingly long ascent that now had her at an altitude of fifty point three kilometres. She could see—blurrily, but very markedly—the world's curvature. Details of the geography below were softened almost beyond recognisability; the multitudinous pencil-stripes of the girdling dunefields had melted into an undifferentiated dark velvet smear. The air above her was brighter, though the lateral visibility was, if anything, worse: she was now high enough to be amidst the lower haze layer. The sun still existed, somewhere low over her left shoulder; she was no longer certain that Saturn did.

The cold was like a skin of ice, leaking into her bones, making her feel that every small inflight judder was bruising her in her seat. Her toes tingled, fingers stung; she wasn't convinced they were still attached to her by limbs. The flight had become a process of merely waiting out – enduring – each individual minute, and the minutes ran overlong. She felt sure, despite the HUD airspeed indicator's evidence to the contrary, that the plane was simply suspended, motionless, in the high ochrous air, like some impotently-animated bug at the tip of a lepidopterist's pin.

'Why so high?' she'd asked the suit. *(Can we afford it?)*

<Our cumulative power consumption is a matter of airspeed, air resistance, cooling rate, and time elapsed. A higher altitude both permits

and requires a higher velocity; air resistance is diminished; loss of mission-critical heat is also diminished. This is the trajectory which offers the greatest probability of success.>

And the most catastrophic outcome upon failure, she'd thought. But had not said.

She should, she thought, be using this "dead time" in contemplation of the Tanja problem, but she could not. Such contemplation was best performed alone, and the cold was an overly-insistent lover that would not let her be. The Skyrider shook a little, hiccupped; the engines' note wobbled around its sonic balance-point; the flight was something that threatened not to end. Or, at any rate, to outlast her.

Then there came a diminution, a simplification of the engine note. The vehicle slowed, started to push its nose sideways. Sideways and down. Through the grimed and streaked windscreen in front of her, she watched the smeary umbered band of the horizon edge up slightly against the plane's streamlined nose. Then the "sideways" ceased, but the "down" persisted. *Descent,* she thought. *Not before time. But—*

The engines' drone, she realised, could not now be heard at all against the rush of dark air whistling around the plane, against the top of her helmet. And the angle of the Volker's descent had increased uncomfortably. There was some turbulence, not the roughest, but probably the most prolonged she'd experienced on the flight. The shaking, slipping, bumping persisted for almost a full minute before the plane slammed through into smooth air. The vehicle was angled down enough that she felt it necessary to tilt her head back, but this disturbed the air pushing over the Volker's windscreen past her helmet, and the plane shuddered. She leaned her head forward, waited it out while the airflow calmed down again.

'Suit,' she said, 'what's happening?'

<Passenger Scarfe. We are in emergency descent mode. Please remain calm.>

'What *kind* of emergency?' she asked. The sheathing cold suddenly nucleated a chill in the pit of her stomach.

<Guerline, please do not be alarmed. I have merely had the plane initiate an emergency-power-only descent – effectively, a low-power glide – so as to apportion as great a quantum of the remaining battery reserves as possible for suit heating. The craft has everything under control. Estimates have us touching down at Trafton Airstation in approximately thirty-eight minutes. For the remainder of the flight, I will be placing my own higher-intellect functions into "sleep" mode to conserve charge. You can still effect communication with the plane, as you have already been doing. I shall re-emerge at the conclusion of our descent, should battery reserves safely permit such a course.>

'Wait,' she said. 'Are the flaps thawed out yet? The ailerons?'

<Guerline, the decision has been taken that the heating required for control-surface activation is not separately available.> The suit paused for long enough that she was convinced it had finished. *<Attitude control will be effected by the distribution and balancing of the craft's eight engines.>*

'This will work?' she asked. The overly formal language, the lack of verbal contractions: it dawned on her that the suit was *worried*.

In which case—

<Turbulence,> the aircraft announced, without even a "Passenger Scarfe" to soften the announcement, as the forward port engine nacelle was – her HUD informed her – taken offline. Then the HUD itself flickered into darkness. The plane ramped into a steeper downward trajectory.

The sudden roughness of the descent had Scarfe fearful for the continued integrity of the small C-fibre aircraft: if something sheared off in this hurtle down through a steadily-thickening atmosphere, she wouldn't be walking away afterwards. 'HUD,' she called, plaintive. 'I need a HUD.'

<Passenger Scarfe, I am working on it,> the Volker assured her. *<However, for the moment there are—>*

'Difficulties?'

<Indeed so.>

Then the HUD was restored, the altitude value dropping so rapidly that the fifth significant figure was just a blur, beyond the capabilities of the HUD's refresh rate. The roar of the harbinger wind almost completely drowned out the motors' slight, higher-pitched whine; the terrain below them, still too indistinct and featureless to seem a direct threat, was ominously placed nonetheless.

The HUD went again, as well as, it seemed, all comms. The shaking had become so violent that she worried, now, about nausea. Nausea in a suit. While the plane was flying blind.

Falling blind, she corrected herself.

The path down stayed lumpy, and the HUD was offline until the twenty-six kilometre mark on the altimeter. *Jesus*, she thought. *We're not even halfway down.*

The immense dunes below were no longer just an undifferentiated blur; they had attained a vague linearity, a striped character. They still appeared effectively flat: just a pattern on the ground, nothing more. The stripes thickened, gained some semblance of contrast.

But she could see, in the dim distance, the dark edge of the dunefields, with paler ice beyond; which meant Trafton was not too much further.

Twenty-five. Twenty-four. Twenty-three. The altimeter edged ever lower.

It occurred to Scarfe that she might yet see a successful end to this flight. If she did not freeze solid in the interim.

<*Brace,*> the plane demanded.

There was nothing she could brace against.

The Skyrider bumped down, bounced alarmingly, skidded with a curdling screech along the groomed but still irregular icy surface of the accessway. Her heart thudded bruisingly against her ribcage, like a trapped animal desperately seeking some means of escape. The props paused, locked, then droned into a multi-throated, discordant reverse. Scarfe was judderingly aware of the speed-streaked banks of dirty-ice rubble that slid past, at still-alarming velocity, not five metres (she thought) from either side of the plane. She didn't like to think of the stress that the aircraft's skid pylons must be under. *If one of those supports should snap, at this speed…*

The cold of her suit magnified every bump, every thump of the plane's rough-scraped landing. The seat restraint, chilled beyond all elasticity, threatened with each small jolt to slice across her suit's chest. She forced herself to breathe slowly; tried to flex her fingers, and was rewarded only with a painful, persistent tingle. The plane was slowing. It started to slew, but some noisy complaint of the tortured props apparently signalled a correction, and it hauled itself true once more. Then, disbelievingly, all was still. Her heartbeat thumped in complaint.

Down.

Now the difficult bit starts.

*

Trafton Emergency kept her for thirty minutes. Perimeter Security detained her for a further ninety, while they pored over her carefully-curated account of the flight, and while she grew ever more keenly aware that she'd eaten nothing since that only-half-finished culturebroth bulb, back in Jeffreys, seven, eight hours ago now. Her head ached, her hands still tingled, her legs threatened to fold under her. And she smiled, and strove to explain once again, to the fourth and then the fifth grim-faced representative of those responsible for maintaining orderly ingress into Trafton, just why she'd overridden the aircraft's safety judgement. When they were unmoved by her pleas of occupational urgency, she played, shamelessly, the parent-of-a-young-child card, and that worked. They were still not happy, but she was a resident, the plane had miraculously not sustained damage, and they were perhaps running out of colleagues to whom to transfer her. They let her go.

Food now? she asked herself. *Or business?*

She started walking, on still-shaking legs, towards the hospital sector.

eight

'You want me to *what?*' N'Diaye asked, pressing his knuckles on the desk as he raised himself from his seat.

'Kim… I would not be asking this if it weren't of paramount importance. A young woman's death is at stake.'

'Exactly. But she's already dead, isn't she?'

'We still don't know *why* she died. Kim, you put so much effort, I know, into seeking to answer the questions behind a death like this. Just extend me the same courtesy.' *It's my job. Even when Kalinda tells me it isn't.*

'Courtesy? You want me to hack the Morgenstein T-suit, to—'

'I'd do it myself, if I had the biometrics.'

'But *I* don't have the biometrics!'

'You've still got Tanja Morgenstein on ice, don't you?' Scarfe asked.

'Well yes, but the privacy concerns—'

'I think Tanja's beyond concerns over bodily privacy by now,' she said. 'But this is central to—' *To clearing her name? Hardly. To uncovering a note intended, in all likelihood, for her mother's eyes alone?* '—to understanding her reasons for choosing death.'

'She's probably beyond understanding the reasons too,' argued N'Diaye. 'This just has "malpractice" written all over it.'

'Kim, we've collaborated for the best part of a decade. Would I ask you to do this on a whim?'

'No,' he said, after a pause. 'No, I don't believe you would. But—'

'It's crucial.' *In deeper*, she thought, and took a long breath. 'And it's Tanja's suit – it's every bit as much a part of the necropsy as she is.'

He sighed. 'It'll take a while. I'll need your signature.'

'Happily,' she said.

'You owe me for this. Big time.'

You may not yet know how big, she thought. The pressure that had been placed on Kalinda, the apparent sabotage of the hired Skyrider, perhaps the obstacle on the Trafton rail approach… they had stopped playing fair very early on, and there was no reason to believe they would change now. She hoped she hadn't opened N'Diaye up to retribution. 'Thank you,' she told him, gratified and awkward.

She crumpled the still-warm insta-soup carton, dropped it in her apartment's cycler.

'I am not to receive any calls,' she instructed the slate, then reconsidered. 'Other than those initiated by Kim N'Diaye. Or Chaim Uchida. Or Sunder or Niki.'

She disliked with a passion the idea of sleep-meds, but she was too wired to manage unassisted rest, and sleep was desperately needed. The door was sealed, she was off the grid… she twisted in her bed, trying to get comfortable, striving to find the key to sleep, wondering if she should take another dose…

… and awoke three hours later, mouth dry, and temporarily utterly disoriented in the darkness of her own bedroom. The slate was flashing a soft, silent alarm. 'What have I missed?' she asked, stumbling to the meal-space basin for a shot of water.

<Message from Dr N'Diaye. And one from Joshua Hainan.>

'What's the gist from Kim?'

<Can you clarify, please?>

She clenched her jaw. 'Summarise the import of the message from Kim N'Diaye. Please.'

<He expressed a strong interest in seeing you. At your earliest convenience. The message from Joshua Hainan—>

'Does it concern a T-suit?'

<That would appear to be among the topics on which he touched, but there was much—>

'I'm not interested in hearing from Joshua Hainan at the moment,' she announced, wondering just where she had left her jacket.

'I don't appreciate being lied to, Guerline,' N'Diaye said, not bothering to stand.

Scarfe remained on her feet: she didn't feel comfortable with taking a seat. His office seemed a much less welcoming space than it had been even five hours ago, and she herself was the reason why.

'Lied to?' she asked, wishing her voice didn't sound so small, so childishly defensive.

'It's not Tanja Morgenstein's suit, is it?'

'It's… possible that it's not,' she conceded. *Have you accessed its memory? Are you going to release the contents to me?* 'Can you seal the door, please?'

He did so, then looked up at her with what she could only describe as a baleful cast to his face. 'It would be thoroughly inappropriate for me to disclose the contents of Yrsa Morgenstein's T-suit to you,' he said. 'There is no way, no way at all, that I, in my position, could be a party to such an action.'

'Of course,' she said woodenly. 'I quite understand that.'

'Because I have refrained from attempting to access the onboard memory of the Morgenstein suit,' he continued, idly pushing a black databud across the desktop towards her, 'I was unable to determine, for example, that the suit has no retinal scanner emplaced within its helmet visor, nor that other key biometric sensors, such as fingerprint readers, are disabled. If I had surmised this, it would have proven necessary to have used the suit's flash DNA sequencing function, virtually its sole active bioidentification protocol, to proceed.'

'That is – or rather, that would have been – a surprising development,' Scarfe acknowledged. *Did Tanja perhaps disconnect those features for ease of use? Which would suggest she may well have used the suit repeatedly.* She stared at the databud before reaching for it.

He placed a proprietary hand over the memory device. 'I'm not done,' he explained. 'Were I to have performed even a cursory examination of the suit's data storage elements, I might have found it difficult, even impossible, to ascertain with any confidence those components connected with Tanja's identity as distinct from those connected to the suit's original occupier. It might seem to me, in the purely hypothetical circumstance that I was wishing to isolate the suit's Tanja Morgenstein-originated data content, as though the two streams of data were blended together for some reason.'

'That would be unexpected,' she said carefully. *This sounds like much more than simply a personal note.*

'Were I to have made a copy of the sum of the suit's stored personal memory' —he pulled his hand back slightly from the data bud, but kept it hovering just above— 'for transfer to some third party for whom the Tanja-related content was professionally relevant…'

'You would require an assurance,' Guerline suggested, 'that said third party would not infringe in any manner on the privacy of that former suit occupant who is not Tanja, by accessing personal data of a non-Tanja origin.'

'An unambiguous assurance,' N'Diaye emphasised.

'Of course,' said Guerline. 'And you would have it.' She dared to pick the databud up.

He did not seek to stop her. 'I hope I have made myself perfectly clear,' he intoned.

'Unambiguously,' she assured him, and, databud in hand, prepared to go.

There was a tone from the door. 'Wait, please,' called N'Diaye, but the door was already sliding open.

If the look N'Diaye had thrown Scarfe's way had been harsh, the one she now received from Yrsa Morgenstein would be best described as venomous. Guerline was painfully aware of the small databud she still held, unconcealed, a red-hot coal in her right hand.

'I really do not see,' said Morgenstein, in clear cold tones that might well have been honed on a whetstone, 'how it can possibly take so long to arrange for the return of my— of family property. You have had that T-suit in your possession for upward of a hundred hours now. How can you still be running tests on it?'

'There is a need to be thorough,' said N'Diaye, choosing to stand. And perhaps, too, sending a signal: from where Morgenstein stood, she would have an unfettered view of his prosthetic legs.

'Do you not,' Scarfe asked, wondering quite how she dared, 'have other T-suits, Ms Morgenstein? More modern ones?' *Perhaps a new one every year or two? Had you even remembered, before Tanja's death, that you still had that one somewhere?*

'That's quite beside the point!' Morgenstein snapped. 'That suit is personal family property, and should be returned immediately. *Immediately.*'

'We have still not completed the trace-element analysis,' said N'Diaye. 'I can give you my full assurance—'

'Kim,' said Scarfe. 'I shouldn't be keeping you. But thanks once again for the results from the Turay throat swab.'

She moved towards – edged past – Morgenstein.

And dropped the databud. Blood rushed to her face, as the small device fell unhurriedly to the floor, not a metre from the other woman's shoe, and bounced back to a resting position just in front of Yrsa Morgenstein.

Before Scarfe could move to retrieve the databud, Morgenstein bent, picked it up. Inspected it with idle half-interest.

And passed it back to Scarfe who, face feeling near-incandescent, muttered, 'Thanks,' and closed her fist around the device.

Scarfe made for the door. She turned from the relative safety of the corridor, called 'Thanks again,' and fled.

Where to? Her residence, suddenly, didn't seem as if it would offer anything approaching sanctuary. Nor did her workspace. She would need time, privacy, security… somewhere… so as to interrogate the databud. 'Personal location encrypted,' she told the slate. She crafted a message, avatar-to-avatar, that would notify Kalinda of her sudden decision to take three days' personal leave, effective immediately.

I could well be wrong, she thought. *But the extent to which Hainan and Kalinda have sought to squash this investigation, the concern Morgenstein expressed over the delayed return of an old, almost-obsolete T-suit… there's something not right with this. Not right at all.*

I can only hope that Tanja's note makes plain the reason for her decision. What could have driven it? What had she become caught in?

Scarfe booked a ticket. Then, before Kalinda could have time to respond to her message, she powered the slate down.

The rail-pod was busier this time than on either of the previous trips. (It was true enough, it would seem, that more people travelled during the week of Titanian daylight than the week of night.) Scarfe wondered at first whether there was even a vacant seat for her; but she found one at the back, on the aisle, beside the oldest child of a noisy and very extroverted family. *Not the ideal environment for detailed or deliberate thought. But perhaps they'll provide useful cover.* She plugged the databud into the slate, activated her device's rarely-used writing surface, and inscribed her instructions. Then she placed the slate in an inner pocket.

The hardest part is the waiting.

Thirty minutes later, the slate shook. She instructed it to manifest an earpiece. But it wasn't the analysis she'd been awaiting.

It was Kim N'Diaye.

He started in without salutation, without any introductory pleasantries. 'This hasn't been publicly released,' he told her. His voice was low, soft, lacking in anything that might pretend to be warmth. 'And if it proceeds to a favourable outcome, it likely won't be. But you might need to know that Yrsa Morgenstein was admitted to intensive care a short time ago. She's currently in an induced coma.'

It took Guerline several seconds to work through the words to their freight. 'What do—'

'She was found with her arm literally coated with somnopatches. If the safeties on the patches hadn't themselves triggered an alarm, she'd probably be… Guerline, what *have* you been stirring up?'

'I wish I knew. Kim, that's awful. Will she pull through?'

'I think it's safest if I not hazard a guess on that score. It's not a certainty, either way.'

'Have you— has there been any reaction from Hainan?'

'I don't think Hainan's been notified. As far as I know, she's cut off all ties to him, filed for annulment a day or two back. Hadn't that information reached you?'

'No, it hadn't. He hasn't *heard*?'

'No. I'd better go.'

She sat in sudden silence, feeling as though she had become sheathed, ice-encased, cordoned off from the pod's other occupants.

Several minutes passed in broody, fruitless, dark-edged contemplation, during which time she asked herself, yet again, why it was that she'd chosen Woltjer as her destination (to which her only answer, unsatisfyingly incomplete, was that *it just feels right*).

Then the slate shook again. She bade it proceed.

< *The T-suit is the property of Yrsa Blaine Morgenstein, and was procured*—>

'I don't need the metadata,' she subvocalised. 'Just a summary of the Tanja-originated contents of the suit's memory.'

<Guerline, there are no such contents.>

The announcement hit her like a wall. *I had been sure she would have left her note in the suit.* Had she co-opted N'Diaye in this exercise for no useful purpose? *Perhaps I do need the metadata after all.* 'But there must be some record, at least, of Tanja's occupation of the suit. She was wearing it when she died.'

<Nonetheless, the suit's records show that the suit's only occupant since purchase has been Yrsa Blaine—>

'That *makes no sense*!'

<Nonetheless, my statements are accurate. External documentation confirms that this is the suit in which Tanja Noor Hainan Morgenstein became deceased. The suit itself, however, maintains that it has only been worn by Yrsa Morgenstein. Guerline, how do you wish me to proceed?>

'I… I don't know,' she confessed. *Had Tanja deleted her own content within the suit? No, she would have had to have done that at death's door, if not posthumously. And what possible reason could anyone else have, to delete her content?*

If all that remains within the suit's memory is Yrsa's property, then I must leave it be. But I was so sure.

I should order the slate to delete its copy of the data…

Instead, she instructed the slate to power down once more. *I need to think. Where did I make the mistake on this?*

Outside the pod, the rough rubbled plains and distant dunefields of western Fensal gave way to the pale, broad, shallow basin that was eastern Xanadu, the only markers in the landscape the mining trackways that led north, to the holdings of the few worthwhile heavy-mineral deposits that could be found in the area. It was, in its way, an attractive stretch of terrain, its bleakness not quite like any other of Titan's bleaknesses.

Scarfe's eyes stared out the viewscreen at the passing scenery: but it would be incorrect to say that she saw any of it.

'Slate?'

<Guerline?>

'Can you summarise for me the most recent ten occasions on which Yrsa Morgenstein's T-suit was occupied?'

<The most recent instance was fourteen hours ago, in the Trafton Medical pathology facility, though at that time only the suit's onboard memory was accessed. This instance ran for six minutes and twenty-two seconds. Previously, the suit was last occupied six days earlier, commencing at the changelocks of the North Trafton Personnel hatch and terminating at the emergency medical facility of Trafton Medical. This instance involved full suit activation including respiration and excretion; loss of respiratory containment occurred when the helmet was unexpectedly detached. Total duration of this instance was one hour and twenty-seven minutes. Prior to this, there was a cluster of six instances scattered across a period of seventeen months, all of which involved full suit activation including respiration, all of which occurred entirely within the confines of the Hainan-Morgenstein residence. These episodes ran for between two hours three minutes and three hours fifty-eight minutes. Before this, there is an interval of nine years and four months during which the suit was not activated at all. The ninth and tenth most recent instances featured durations of, respectively, two days eight hours and thirty-eight minutes

and four days sixteen hours and forty-four minutes, including respiration, ingestion, excretion, medication, navigation and communication, and ranged over a considerable portion of southern Hotei Regio.>

'Is there extant stored memory resulting from these… instances? Beyond just the metadata?'

<There is.>

'For which instances?'

<For all instances. But Guerline, the identified occupant in all instances was Yrsa Morgenstein.>

I don't care what the slate says, I don't care what the suit says, that can't *be right. The most recent of those was N'Diaye, using Tanja's biometrics to spoof her ID. And the time before that was Tanja, dying. But the two oldest times, the long excursions around Hotei, that sounds like geochem, which does sound like Yrsa.* 'Wait. Did Yrsa Morgenstein acquire a new T-suit about, what, eleven years ago, around or shortly after the time of those Hotei walkabouts?'

<If this suit's memory contains such information, it's among Yrsa Morgenstein's personal data, to which access on my part would be inappropriate.>

Damn. 'What about in public-access images? Can you identify a switch in Yrsa's T-suits around this time?'

<I will investigate. Please hold.>

Scarfe counted down softly from one hundred. She'd reached eighty-eight when the slate chimed. 'Well?'

<The imagery is consistent with your hypothesis. For the Hotei Arcus fieldwork, she wore a Hainan model G3-X suit. For subsequent fieldwork in Tui Regio, Arrakis Planitia, and Hobal Virga, commencing the following month and encompassing seventy-eight instances spanning

twenty-two months, she wore a Hainan model G4-M. For the mining campaign at Rossak Planitia, over an interval of twenty-five months, she wore a suit which appears to be a Hainan model H55-B, though I surmise that it may have been customised to some degree. For the interval—>

'That's plenty. Thank you. Power down.'

That isn't Morgenstein's suit anymore. Well, in law, perhaps, but not in fact. I would lay strong odds that those tryouts at the Hainan-Morgenstein residence were Tanja as well – and I would bet, also, that they occurred while both Hainan and Morgenstein were away on work, either at Jeffreys or out on fieldwork somewhere. And come to think of it, by then Piotr would have moved to Sagan as well. So Tanja was taking advantage of a sporadic window of opportunity.

But the suit thought, every time, that Tanja was Yrsa. Why would it think that?

The biometrics wouldn't match. There'd be commonalities, but not enough…

N'Diaye said it was the DNA reader that got him in. But Tanja's DNA wouldn't—

Oh.

'Slate?'

<Guerline?>

Was it Scarfe's imagination, or was there a hint of how-dare-you-keep-toggling-me-off-and-on in the device's synthesised tones? She whispered in a voice barely consistent with the device's auditory sensitivity. 'I need the suit's data dating from its second most recent instance of use, that is, the time consistent with the occasion of Tanja Morgenstein's death.' *If there's a note, that's when it would have been set down.*

<Access to, and analysis of, the memory parcel you indicate is not consistent with the terms of your investigation. The suit's stored data remains the private property of its user, Yrsa Blaine Morgenstein.>

'That's only technically true, and only because the suit failed to identify Tanja as the suit's most recent occupant. Please extricate the indicated data.'

<Guerline, the protected memory is clearly flagged as the intellectual property of Yrsa Blaine Morg—>

'That is an error of attribution. That data is Tanja's. Please extricate the data.' *Don't stonewall me on this.*

<You are instructing this device to act in contravention of the established norms of data privacy?>

'Yes.'

<You are in possession of reasonable and defensible grounds, obtained lawfully within the execution of your responsibilities as an official acting on behalf of Fensal prefecture, to assert that such contravention by this device is in the greater good?>

A second's hesitation. 'Yes.'

<You will indemnify this device against all legal responsibility for the breach you are requesting?>

'Indeed so,' she asserted, feeling a rising level of frustration with the device. 'I authorise this in accordance with my legal responsibility to investigate comprehensively such factors regarding Tanja Morgenstein's death as may be considered to reasonably impinge on the collective ongoing functionality and productivity of Fensal's society.' It was difficult to clearly enunciate the required boilerplate text fully under her breath, and once again a few of the nearer passengers turned their heads in her direction. But the slate appeared satisfied.

Some seconds elapsed. 'Well?'

<Guerline?>

'How long will this take?'

<I cannot be sure. Those data are protected.>

'How so?'

<The memory parcel is marked for the attention of "My Mother Yrsa".>
Yes! 'But?'

<It is passcode protected. The passcode reads "Why be so secretiv?", omitting the final "e" of "secretive".>

'Display it.'

It was as the slate described.

<It requires a correct response for access. Guerline, how should I proceed?>

'Is there any context given for the passcode's question?'

<Only that the memory parcel is marked for the attention of "My Mo—>

'Is there any way in which you can circumvent this passcode?'

<Not that I can ascertain. How should I proceed?>

'Power down.'

"Why be so secretiv?"

It could mean anything.

The pod had another five hours, almost six, to go until it reached Woltjer. She stared, not-seeing, at the scenery streaming past. *It's an open-ended question, but it requires a precise answer. Something Yrsa Morgenstein would know.*

What did Tanja know, that her mother did not want her to know? And why the missing final "e"?

She could feel a tension headache developing.

She forced herself to get up and go in search of food.

nine

Neve seemed almost childishly happy to see her. Guerline consented to a stifling, almost one-sided hug, but managed, towards the end of the embrace, to make some overtures towards reciprocity. Thanh, in whose presence Guerline Scarfe had always felt awkward and apologetic, smiled and shook her hand. They walked, three abreast, the short distance from the terminus concourse to the restaurant section, with Neve insistent on holding Guerline's hand, her bag pressing and bumping repeatedly against Guerline's hip. *Freyne.*

I shouldn't be encouraging this, Scarfe told herself, once again, though more out of duty than conviction; she felt powerless to do anything that might upend Neve's fragile, hard-won equilibrium. Aloud she asked, 'So are you still in that basement unit on the southern edge?'

It was to Neve that the question was clearly directed, but it was Thanh who answered, for his mute friend. 'Yes, Freyne likes it there.' It no longer sounded strange – at least, not more than marginally so, and the impression didn't linger – to hear Neve's words in Thanh's voice, but Guerline could not help but wonder, still, what it was that Thanh derived from the interaction. Were they linked romantically, yet, as well as functionally? It was plain that he adored Neve: at least, it was plain to Guerline, though she wondered, sometimes, if the other saw it. It was possible Neve was so enmeshed with Freyne, still, that she just could not perceive anything else. *Anything more real,* Guerline thought to herself, and could not, for all her might, unthink it; it felt treacherous, holding Neve's hand in this manner.

It was what it was; or what it seemed. And Neve was not her client, but her friend. And a connection to something now dead, something still tender.

The rest of the walk – past bright-lit stores and galleries, a colour-clashing row of business offices, and a park scarcely big enough to contain the water feature that comprised its centrepiece – passed in silence. It was a companionable silence, unhurried, assured. At least, that was Guerline's experience of it; but who was she to tell?

They arrived at the restaurant. They made their way inside, through the soft-lit, coolly-damp fernery that might, or might not, be genuinely botanical; Guerline brushed her hand against a couple of fronds on the way in, and remained none the wiser.

Why be so secretiv?

There were so many possible answers to that, and only one correct.

The servitor guided them to their booth, asked if they wished to opacify the viewpanel. They asked for it to remain lightly frosted: the restaurant's lighting was a little dim, and the panel gave (for Guerline and Neve, at least) a good view of the park's small fountain and pool.

They placed the usual order. Guerline had the yearning to try something new, but she knew this wouldn't sit well with Neve, for whom the ritual was important.

She stared, in what she hoped conveyed more a look of appreciation and familiarity than of curiosity, at Neve's face, once so perfectly symmetrical, now marked with the scars, predominantly on her right side, that ran from her hairline to the base of her jaw. But the damage was old, comfortable: *heritage* scars, she thought to herself. And it was a face that looked happy, at least for the moment. It no longer hurt, much, to look on Neve's circlet-capped face, just as it was no longer so painful to meet Kim N'Diaye, to rekindle those links to Freyne, her brother. It no longer bit quite so severely to think back to that disastrous expedition several years past, amongst the peaks of Mithrim, on which five had set out and only three had returned. She no longer wished Neve healed, the damage undone: Neve was as healed as she was going to get, and if she was happy – and Thanh assured her that, for the most part, she was – then what remained was not Guerline's problem. Scarfe couldn't even begrudge her the name Neve had chosen for the doll in her bag; Neve was a link to Guerline's past, or a part of that past, and a reminder that, in some shape, life proceeded. It was a reminder she still needed, more often than she'd wish.

She longed to put all this in words, but she knew she dared not. Not to Neve, for she quite lacked Neve's brave unguardedness; she always had. Perhaps she'd express it in a letter sometime, worded with care and regard, though she knew this to be an empty promise. She turned to Thanh, asked after his work, his parents. Easy stuff. Conversation took hold.

Then Thanh's long, handsome face – like Neve's, topped by a slender C-fibre circlet – grew serious, and he seemed to collect himself before saying, 'It's so good to see you again, Guerline.' She knew, from his face, from the slight shift in his voice, from Neve's unspoken intensity of expression, that the words weren't his but Neve's, transmitted from one to the other through those circlets. (It wasn't a choice Guerline would ever have made herself, the implants and the hardware required for 'functional telepathy' in preference to the reconstruction or repair of the speech centre and vocal cords. But she could understand, on one level, why Neve had selected it: her voice had been perfect before. Post-reconstruction, she was never going to recapture the purity of those earlier performances.)

'I'm glad I could be here, Neve,' she replied, and she meant it.

Their mains arrived, and they got busy with their meals. As always, Thanh's lack of dexterity with his chopsticks became a running joke, and Neve at one point, expressing *faux* concern for his nutritional wellbeing, deftly cantilevered a morsel off her own plate into his mouth. A look passed between them, private, warm. Perhaps more than a look, for who but they knew what the circlets encoded and decoded? Guerline focussed on the bowl in front of her.

And spelled something out, for perhaps the hundredth time, in her own mind.

And stood up. *The missing "e". Of course it was a code. And Yrsa Morgenstein is a geochemist.* 'Sorry,' she told them, still trying to think back through something she'd been taught long ago. 'I'll be back in a minute.'

The restaurant's restroom was clean – sparkling, even – but it stank. Someone in the other cubicle hadn't flushed. It couldn't be helped.

'Slate?'

<Guerline?>

'The passcode question. They're element symbols. From the periodic table. "W" is tungsten, "H" is hydrogen, "Y" is yit-something—'

<Yttrium.>

'Yes, that one… and there's no way for "secretive" to end in "e", so it's missing that letter.'

<That is a plausible alternate framing of the question – but then, what is the answer? The combination of elements is not suggestive of a process.>

'Try the element numbers.'

<The atomic numbers.>

'Yes, those. Tanja wouldn't have been looking to make the question unsolvable, but she wanted her mother to sweat over finding the answer.' *Which implies anger, on Tanja's part. Why so?*

<That appears to have satisfied the requirements. The memory parcel is now unlocked. Do you wish to inspect the contents? There are seventy-six individual files.>

'I'm with friends; I'll examine them later. Power down.'

They opted not to have dessert, though Guerline felt tempted. To distract herself, she told Neve, 'I brought a small toy for Freyne,' and she reached into her bag, retrieving the little cryocrawler kit, smaller brother to the one Nikita had yet to receive.

Neve's face grew radiant, her smile almost alarmingly wide. 'Oh, *thank you*,' said Thanh's voice, with such sincerity and depth of emotion that Guerline almost felt upstaged, here with her childhood friends – and her brother's bereaved, still-troubled lover – by a mere toy. Neve took Freyne – the doll Freyne, the eponymous onetime possession of Guerline's brother – from her bag and cradled doll and cryocrawler kit on her lap. 'Freyne *loves* this,' announced Thanh, and Guerline, feeling vicariously self-conscious, watched for a few seconds with a mixture of awkwardness and tenderness until her friend put the doll and toy back in her bag.

'I'm glad,' said Guerline, and was moderately surprised to learn that this was true. *People cope however they can*, she told herself.

I have good friends, I should try to be less distant. But it was difficult. Her mind kept dragging her in unhelpful, sometimes troubling directions. As it had just now.

If Tanja Morgenstein is her mother's daughter – and only *her mother's daughter, born very late into a family troubled by infertility – then who is, or who was, Tanja's brother Piotr?*

ten

She had expended so much of the past week in travel; and for what? She wasn't sure, still, what it amounted to. Was it really the case that the face-to-face contact conveyed genuinely better access to the body language, the small personal "tells" of her interviewees? Or was it that the reprieve from routine afforded her the opportunity to explore connections of which she would otherwise have remained ignorant? It was probably both.

The pod wasn't as packed, this time, as it had been yesterday, but it was still sufficiently busy that she hadn't been able to get a seat without neighbours. The man beside her was older, business-attired. She responded briefly to his conversational overtures, but let it be known without, she hoped, appearing rude, that she wasn't interested in an extended dialogue with a stranger.

She didn't dare activate the slate: with several other passengers within close proximity, she hadn't yet carved out for herself the personal space necessary. Instead, she watched the scenery slide past the pod viewscreen. She'd always enjoyed this first stretch of the Woltjer-to-Trafton run, with its streambeds and its embankments sculpted from Titan's tholin-rusted icy bedrock. She dozed a little, despite herself, and roused at some subtle shift in the pod's motion: the broad bend southeast that averted any incursion by west Fensal's dark dunefields into the pod's route. Still substantially less than halfway from Woltjer; still seven or more hours before she would be home. The businessman beside her had his head turned away, either watching the scenery or drowsing.

She took the slate out, patched herself in. Asked for its report.

Tanja's note to her mother was churlish in its brevity. It read, simply: *I found out.*

There were many other items in the parcel, some of which Scarfe had neither use for nor any right to know. Personal details on Yrsa Morgenstein's health, finances, sexual history. A full record of Yrsa's long recourse to rejuvenation treatments. There was, though, after that, final confirmation of Tanja as a sole genetic replicate of Yrsa. *A clone.* And a confidential report, signed by the same geneto-specialist, identifying Piotr Hainan as a sole genetic replicate of his father, Joshua Hainan. And then there was—

'Wait,' she said, aloud, and the businessman looked up, shifted in his seat, glanced towards her. She made an apologetic hand gesture; after several long seconds, he turned back to his perusal of the landscape. She exhaled, inhaled. Muttered, in the quietest tones she could muster, 'Identify Isandro Ashkenazy.'

<Doctor Isandro Poul Ashkenazy is a surgical transplant specialist, recently retired, formerly indentured to South Sagan Emergency Medical Facility. He has expertise in the areas of…>

Scarfe felt the environment grow ten degrees colder as she listened to the slate's poorly-modulated tones in her earpiece. The notion which had just insinuated itself into her mind was too awful to give credence to. And yet, like a black hole, it had its own unassailable gravity.

You've gone in too deep, Guerline. There's no climbing out now.

But, as ideas spun off from the central, unforgiving revelation, new connections made themselves known. 'Whereabouts of the remains of Piotr Hainan,' she whispered, hoping – or at least half-hoping – she was wrong. The slate's response told her she wasn't: Piotr Hainan lay exactly where she expected him to be.

How convenient for his father, she thought.

She might still be wrong. She got up to visit the pod's restroom.

She planted herself on the white C-fibre lid of the pod's sole commode, arranged a call. Voice and image for this one.

'Zeera?' she asked the slate. 'Guerline Scarfe. I'm calling from— I want to check something with you. It relates to your time with Piotr Hainan.'

'That was more than two years ago,' Kwan protested, her voice and her unkempt appearance both suggesting that Scarfe's call may have woken her up.

'Understood. I'm sorry to intrude on your time. But I'd like you to think back, as best you can, as to whether Piotr ever told you about any childhood illness he had, any major childhood illness that may have required surgery to, to his face.'

'I really don't... no, wait, actually I think there was. I think he said that, when he was very small, he had surgery to deal with a serious asthma issue. Just like—'

'Like Tanja,' said Scarfe, and a chill akin to liquid methane ran down her back. Yrsa Morgenstein's health history was clear of any mention of asthma, which implied that Tanja should not have carried any susceptibility. And she was willing to bet that Joshua Hainan's medical records would be similarly clean of the condition. *Did they use surgery as a way to disguise their children's identities as single-parent replicates?* 'Zeera, this is important. Are you *sure* about this?'

'I think so,' Kwan said, slowly, carefully. 'Sorry. It was a long time ago. And we never talked much about childhood stuff – at least he never did. But yes, I think I remember him telling me about this. It might even have been his earliest memory. He didn't like the hospital, found it scary. Made him cry.' On the screen, Kwan twisted her neck slightly, stifled a yawn. 'What does this have to do with Tanja's death?'

'I'm just looking to exclude some possibilities. I can't be more specific than that, unfortunately.'

'Oh.'

'Did he ever tell you about any holidays he'd been on with his parents? Before the trip to Ligeia?'

'I don't think so. No. Yes, he was always resentful that his parents would go places, and leave him behind.'

'Was that a frequent happening? Their travelling?'

'Ms Scarfe,' Kwan said, with her eyes narrowed and her voice highly guarded. 'I really don't see what this has to do—'

'It's not something I'm in a position to explain. But I can assure you that I have Tanja's best interests at heart. Thank you for talking with me, Zeera, it's greatly appreciated. I won't take up any more of your time.' She terminated the call.

She stared at the small cubicle's blank door, but she wasn't seeing anything in the room. She was seeing… horrid images, unspeakable betrayal. The worst betrayal, she thought, that one human could inflict on another. And, finally, she'd reached that place, that cold cold place, where she had no doubt about why Tanja Morgenstein took her own life. And why Tanja's mother may have sought to follow her.

It was too much. She wanted to leave it here, in this cubicle, to just walk away, forget it all. But she couldn't do that. She'd never be able to do that.

She made another call. His face grew guarded as he recognised her. The reaction gave her a pang, but she pressed on. 'Sunder, hi,' she said. 'Is everything alright?'

'As far as I know,' he replied. 'Guerline, why are you calling?'

'Is Nikita with you?'

'He's simming in the other room. Do you want a word with him?'

'Better not. Just… it's probably a good idea to keep him close for the next twelve hours or so, until I'm back. And keep him away from his slate. There's some stuff I have to do, and I'd rather he found out from me than from any other source.'

'What are you talking about?'

'I can't go into that.' She was finding it difficult to stop her voice from shaking. 'But there's a chance – quite a good chance – it could all blow up.'

'Keep him from his slate? Guerline, I told you, he's simming right now.'

'Then wean him off it, just for tonight, and tomorrow. Please. Play vehicles with him or something, he'll enjoy that. Tell him I… I'll take him to the N-pool, the day after tomorrow.'

'I had plans of my own.'

'Please, Sunder. I wouldn't be asking this if it wasn't important. I know you've been hearing that from me a lot these past few days. But this is coming to a head.'

'*What's* coming to a head? Guerline, what the hell are you mixed up in?'

'Some client stuff has got messy,' she said. 'I can't tell you more than that right now. You'll probably be able to put two and two together by tomorrow, but I don't want Niki doing that. Please?'

'There had better be a damn good reason for this.'

'A good reason? I can't really judge that. But I know I... this is something I must do. And I need your help with Niki.'

'*Damn* it, Guerline... yes, very well. But there had better be an explanation forthcoming.'

'Sunder, thank you. There will be. I do appreciate this. I'll see you tomorrow.'

'Take care,' he told her, with that reluctant tone in his voice that conveyed all too clearly his resentment.

She closed the call. She exhaled heavily, held herself still for a half-minute. Trying not to think.

It didn't work; it never did.

Then she asked the slate, 'If I place a call from here, full privacy, can my location be traced?'

<Guerline, the best time to have asked that would have been before the call.>

'I'm not talking about the calls I've just made. I'm talking about the next one. Just answer the question.'

<I do not believe so.>

'You don't *believe* it can be traced?'

<Guerline, I cannot be entirely certain. There are capabilities to which I'm not privy. But on the balance of probability, I think not.>

She sighed. *The balance of probability will have to do*. 'Right. Place a call, full privacy. Priority. Voice only.' Took a deep breath. 'It's time I returned Joshua Hainan's calls.'

eleven

He took his time answering, his voice sleep-slurred. She felt a small victory at that. 'Guerline Scarfe,' she explained.

'The investigator,' he replied. 'But what—'

She'd keep this short. 'I know about Ashkenazy,' she told him. Then reminded herself that she was dealing with a bully, a corporate aggressor, and someone much more malevolent than his public persona. A closet psychopath. An instigator of murder.

Such people were clever, and accustomed to getting their way. Whatever advantage Joshua Hainan's somnolent haze conferred on her, it wouldn't last long.

She marshalled her inner fire. Loaded as much hate, as much contempt, as she could into her tone. 'You got yours, isn't that right?' she asked. She saw in her mind's eye those old eyes, those young hands. 'You got *yours*, and she didn't get *hers*, isn't it so? She was never going to, now. *That's* why she kept shying away from you in the interview. You sick, sick bastard.'

She terminated the call just as he started to reply.

She was shaking, her palms wet. Her heart raced. And someone was thumping on the cubicle door.

'No calls whatsoever,' she told the slate, her voice quaking. 'No outside contact, not from Sunder, not from Kalinda, not from *anybody*, until my express authorisation.' She stood up, quickly composed herself, opened the door. Was met by an irate father holding the hand of a small boy, perhaps half Nikita's age, whose face bore the unmistakable stamp of barely-contained desperation.

She muttered an apology and eased herself out past the queue.

twelve

The slate informed her that there were still five hours remaining of the ride back to Trafton. She wanted the journey done, *now*, but of course she needed to wait it out.

She used the time to put it all down. Two children, raised from birth – or rather, from creation – for just one single ultimate purpose, their faces modified through adaptive surgery ("childhood asthma") to disguise their true identity: their true genetic nature. The months of weight loss Hainan had had to go through, in the lead-up to Ligeia, so as to be a match, a comparable physique, to his son. The carelessness of Yrsa Morgenstein in not wiping the onboard memory, not disabling the data-synch feature, from a decade-old T-suit. A suit which had mistakenly identified Tanja Morgenstein as her own mother, and had thus accorded her full access to Yrsa's stored information.

The lakesuited body of "Piotr Hainan" – though not, in truth, Piotr Hainan, or at least not *mostly* – discarded in one of the deepest reaches of Ligeia Mare, effectively beyond retrieval.

Parents who would *do* such a thing – and that was something she just could not get her head around, no matter how much she tried (and a mental image of Nikita, here, brought her almost to tears) – merely for the prospect of a few decades of life extension. (And then what? A repetition of the whole grim sequence?)

And a worlds-renowned surgeon, bought at God only knew what price, possessing among his skills set the ability to perform head transplants.

Younger bodies. For when the rejuvenation treatments lost their effectiveness. Her stomach clenched at the thought, and she forced herself to swallow, to breathe more slowly. Nausea was averted – she thought – but lacrimation, it turned out, could not be dispelled. Her face ached with the strain of it.

Scarfe longed to be able to find the time, the space, to properly grieve a young woman she had met too late, a young woman who, having learned the devastating truth of her intended fate, had seen no way of escape from the clutches of a powerful, almost all-pervasive family. No way out, except the most desperate; undertaken in such a way as to deny her own mother the thing she'd most craved. Scarfe wondered if she had done enough to protect Tanja's lover, Chaim Uchida, by encrypting all record of his disclosures to her. Probably not. There was a strong possibility that the report she was about to send, to Kim N'Diaye, to her own supervisors, to South Sagan Emergency Medical Facility, to Sagan Admin, to Titan Northern Lakes Region health section, to the Trafton constabulary, and to Joshua Hainan himself – he'd see it anyway, so may as well give him everything – would not, in any way, ameliorate anything for anybody alive. But sometimes one owed the dead a greater responsibility than the living. And Guerline Scarfe appreciated this more strongly than most, by virtue of her occupation.

'*Send,*' she told the slate, suspecting that she'd just killed her career. She put the slate away, rummaged further within her bag, needing – and, after a few seconds, obtaining – the tactile reassurance of the cryocrawler kit which she would soon give to her son. She mourned the lost simplicity, the clarity, of childhood.

The rail-pod slid on, smooth as ever, towards Trafton, and Nikita, still three hours away.

acknowledgements

The worldbuilding in this story has benefitted from the feedback I've received from many people on this and on other Titan stories I've worked on over the past decade. Thanks are due to the participants in CSFG crit group sessions in which those stories featured, and to the editors who selected the stories for magazines and anthologies. Particular thanks are owed to the brave individuals, Dion Perry and Rob Porteous, who have proofread this story.

I'm profoundly grateful to 'Looey' (Lewis P Morley) for once again providing a stunning cover image.

I'm also deeply indebted to Edwina Harvey, whose editorial interventions have, as always, improved the telling.

Any defects that remain in the text – and there are bound to be some, for this isn't an ideal universe – are, of course, my own responsibility.

about the author

Born and raised in North Canterbury, New Zealand, Simon Petrie now lives in Canberra, Australia, with his books, his occasional ongoing forays into scientific research, and his least-effort plans for galactic domination. His short fiction has appeared in numerous places; much of it has been conveniently corralled into two now inconveniently out-of-print short fiction collections *Rare Unsigned Copy* and *Difficult Second Album*. He has been shortlisted several times for the Sir Julius Vogel, Ditmar, and Aurealis Awards, and he has won the Sir Julius Vogel Award three times: in 2010 for Best New Talent and in 2013 and 2018, with *Flight 404* and *Matters Arising from the Identification of the Body* respectively, for Best Novella. He also scored a coveted Dishonourable Mention in the 2011 Bulwer-Lytton Fiction Contest.

He has edited five issues (numbers 35, 40, 51, 54, and ~~bingo~~ 61) of *Andromeda Spaceways Inflight Magazine*, and has co-edited two anthologies (*Light Touch Paper, Stand Clear* and *Use Only As Directed*, published by Peggy Bright Books) with Edwina Harvey and one (*Next*, published by CSFG Publishing) with Rob Porteous. He's also acted as a typesetter and e-book formatter for several small-press and indie publishers in Australia and North America. He is currently a member of the Canberra Speculative Fiction Guild and SpecFicNZ writers' communities.

Guerline Scarfe returns, next year, in

a reappraisal
of the circumstances resulting in death

Turn the page for a brief preview…

one

The ride from Turtle had been sufficiently challenging, for both herself and the skid-bike, that Prabha's servo'd wrists ached by the time she pulled to a halt outside the installation. The W&E Afekan Command Centre, a thirty-metre-diameter prefab geodome, heavily stained and almost completely devoid of windows, was crouched on the broad, weathered eastern rim of the crater. In pale full sun, as now, the track leading up the crater wall was wide enough that the ascent didn't intimidate so much as tire, but she wouldn't have liked to negotiate it during the week of night. The access road hewn into the ice-rock of the crater wall had been marred and rutted by the repeated passage of heavy tracked vehicles – as generally happened, she supposed, with mining operations – and the road's inner shoulder, where the surface was generally smoother and thus more accommodating to the skid-bike, was frequently choked by sticky drifts of umber-coloured, coarse-grained hydrocarbon sand.

Looking westward, the tholin-stained, intermittently sand-choked crater wall sloped down unhurriedly, in a haphazard, age-eroded jumble towards Afekan's sand-strewn floor, a couple of hundred metres below. Prabha thought she could just espy a couple of lighter, blocky, clearly artificial obtrusions in the intermediate distance, though it was not apparent whether they were vehicles or buildings.

There were other obtrusions, larger, less regular – weathered hillocks and ridges, she presumed, daubed in the false shade of their tholined crusting – scattered elsewhere across the crater floor. Distance, or the staining on her helmet's visor – or possibly a conspiracy of the two – robbed her of any hint of the crater's far wall, more than a hundred kilometres away.

In the absence of any apparent visitor parking, she pushed the skid-bike across to the geodome's western perimeter, voice-locked it, and went in search of an airlock.

The air stank. She should probably have expected that.

'Khalil, can you please get me those— Oh.' The woman who emerged through the front office hatchway was big, not so much tall as solid, her shortsleeved tunic displaying the most heavily muscled arms Prabha had ever seen. Broad face, green eyes beneath thick brows, soot-black shoulder-length hair. Orca tattoo on her right arm. Voice higher-pitched than seemed in keeping with her build, her bearing.

Prabha stepped forward, awkwardly holding her daypack, its handle still carrying some residue of Titan-chill, in her left hand while she extended the other to shake. 'Agent Prabha Braun, Turtle pol,' she said. 'You'd reported some kind of problem?'

What followed, Prabha felt, was less a handshake than an exercise in digitally-mediated constriction. 'Ulla Frick,' the older woman explained, releasing the pressure. 'Supervisor. Are the others still outside?'

'Others?' asked Prabha. 'I don't—'

'Is it just you?' asked Frick. 'No offence, but...'

'Just what kind of problem had you reported?'

Frick's eyes narrowed, and she gave a small quick exhalation before breathing in, more deeply and slowly. 'You'd better come through to the lab.'

'Right.' Prabha followed Frick through a hatchway to the right of the office, and along a short corridor. 'My suit's still in the airlock. Is that likely to pose a difficulty?'

'I doubt anyone's going to steal it,' Frick replied, not bothering to turn around. 'If that's what you mean.'

'Fine. And is there anywhere around here I can get it freshened?'

Ulla Frick's answering laugh was, Prabha thought, more symptomatic of derision than of mirth.

The hatchway they stopped at bore on its door the inexpertly-stencilled label "GEOCHEM", as well as several scuffs and scratches of sufficient prominence for Prabha to harbour doubts as to its continued utility as an emergency pressure barrier. Frick gave the briefest of courtesy knocks before pushing her palm against the admit panel.

Prabha wasn't sure what she had been expecting from the laboratory – probably something like the stereotypical scene in sims she'd partaken of – but this wasn't it. A couple of large, and by no means new-looking, black cabinets dominated one side of the room; a hip-high workbench, on which were sprawled flimsies, reagent canisters, and a pile of emergency masks, stretched the length of the opposite side. Pipes, ducts, and cables ran up the far wall and across the ceiling. Above all this – overlaid upon it, suffusing it, helping somehow to define it – was the sharp sweet stink of Titan ice.

A small man, in bright, overly-tight clothes – green top, red and blue trousers – was hunched over some blockish-looking instrument at the far end of the workbench, worrying it with an oligotool. He did not look up as they entered.

'You seen Khalil anywhere?' Frick asked.

Now he did glance up, double-took at the sight of Prabha. Elfin features, stubble, a scar on his left cheek that ran almost up to his eye. Big meaty hands. 'Thought he'd been to see you earlier.'

'He didn't find me,' said Frick.

'And this is…?'

'Agent Braun, from Turtle pol.' Frick turned briefly to Prabha, as though to confirm these particulars, before turning back to the figure at the workbench. 'She's here in response to the… incident.' With this, the supervisor backed out of the room.

Well, thought Prabha, wondering what happened next. The lab's heating kicked in with an aggressive whirr.

'How much has Ulla told you about this?' the lab worker asked her after a few awkward seconds.

'Not much,' replied Prabha, raising her voice so as to remain audible over the heat-pump's turbines. 'Suppose you just tell me everything you think is relevant, in your own words? And I regret, I didn't catch your name…'

'Bo Culbertson. Geochemistry.' He placed the oligotool on the bench and moved toward her, hand outstretched.

What is it with these people and death-grip handshakes? she wondered. 'Look, to be perfectly frank, I haven't been briefed on this at all. Whatever information may have been transmitted to Turtle pol

4

about this incident hasn't been relayed to me. So I'd be grateful if you can tell me why pol attention was sent for.'

'It's probably best if I show you,' he said, pausing the climate control before crossing to the farther cabinet. Opened, its black door (emblazoned, she now saw, with a contrasting decal that declared "Frozen Oceanography Practised Here") almost completely blocked the gap between cabinets and bench, and quite eclipsed Culbertson, of whom the only trace, for the moment, was a sequence of shuffling and scampering sounds as he searched for something among the cabinet's shelves. 'Ah.' He placed an object on the bench, closed up the cabinet—the heat pump rumbled into action again—and then he gingerly carried his find over to Prabha. Resting in the slight concavity of a disposable plastic sample tile was a rough chunk of something about two centimetres across, some mineral, she guessed: a light greyish-brown, and with a crumbled texture to much of its surface. He prodded it gently with the oligotool, revealing darker brown shading on its underside. 'We pulled this out of the masticator runoff, down on the crater floor. There was a fair bit more of it, too, as well as the other stuff you'd expect.'

'I'm sorry, I don't... what is it exactly, that you're showing me?'

His eyes flicked from her, to the sample, back to her again. 'It's bone,' he said. 'Human bone.'

want more titan fiction?

Light levels are low. It's killingly cold. These conditions are, it transpires, connected.

The icy landscape around you—hillocks, boulders, ravines, foregrounding a hazy, rumpled horizon beneath an opaque, lowering sky—wears a patina that shades from sepia to umber, puddled with drifts of dark sand. The atmosphere, though thick, would permit only a parody of respiration: there is no succour in it. Were it not for the insulating, carefully-regulated containment of your suit, you would be dead within minutes, frozen solid within an hour.

Welcome to Titan.

Simon Petrie's *Wide Brown Land: stories of Titan*, out now, is a collection of eleven hard-SF short stories set on the same Titan that Guerline Scarfe calls home.

www.ingramcontent.com/pod-product-compliance
Lightning Source LLC
Chambersburg PA
CBHW021432110726
47901CB00008B/2395